The Linden Tree & the Legionnaire

Article 58

Diana Mathur

Dedicated to
Kārlis

Nevermind how she came by her vintage jewelry.

Featuring the paintings of Latvian Legionnaire
Kārlis Smiltens

Corporal Smiltens has donated
over two hundred drawings and paintings
to the Latvian War Museum in Riga.

Article 58

1940 Latvia, perilously positioned between two
maniacal, totalitarian dictatorships.

Prologue

THE SUMMERHOUSE, LATVIA
MIDSUMMER'S EVE, 1992

"I AM KĀRLIS PĒRKONS," KĀRLIS *called, peering down into the root cellar. "This is my house."*

The man in the suit was squatting on the cellar floor, examining a shovel at the body's head. He looked up at Kārlis, and ordered, "Don't go anywhere, old man."

Kārlis straightened up stiffly and looked around. Root cellar access was just outside the kitchen door. The dozen assorted police officials tromping through the house and property disturbed him, the green, tangled overgrowth of spring at odds with a corpse. He breathed deeply, calmed by the verdant earth, especially Latvian soil. All had gone as planned until now, he reassured himself. This too would be handled in the proper order.

Kārlis moved aside for men in blue jumpsuits carrying a stretcher. They paused at the cellar entrance, a wooden rectangular frame that jutted up from the ground at an angle, and started to descend the steep, narrow steps. The cellar door lay where it had been flung in the surrounding tall grass, rotted right off the hinges.

"Don't trust those stairs," Kārlis told them. "They're decrepit."

Kārlis walked to where the police cars and ambulance were parked, and waited. Emergency lights pulsed red over the summerhouse's crumbling plaster and stone edging. Minutes later, the man in the suit, a detective, emerged from the cellar and approached Kārlis, flipping his notepad.

"Hmph. Private property," the detective said. He had a Russian accent, dripping with sarcasm. "And you, the owner."

It was more a jeer than a question, so Kārlis didn't answer. He was an obvious westerner, the only one in town dressed in pastels and running shoes.

"You waited a long time to get your hands on the place," the detective said. "Most people in your position have given up."

"I always kept the paperwork in order," Kārlis replied.

A police officer with tall black boots and handcuffs dangling from his belt strode over to where they stood and addressed the detective. "The victim, name: Igor Volkov, lived here. Retired KGB."

"That's Volkov?" Kārlis said, pointing at the root cellar. "Ak tu kungs."

"Oh, my lord," the detective mimicked. "Yah. That is Volkov. Murdered in your private root cellar. Did you and the victim argue?"

Kārlis said nothing. He wouldn't call a lifelong vendetta an argument. During his silence, birds screamed, reveling in the extended hunting of the prolonged dusk, kids yelled playfully, a distant firecracker popped.

"All right, Pērkons," the detective said. "We'll talk at the station."

Kārlis nodded. "I'll get my jacket," he said, heading toward the kitchen door.

Kārlis would not get in a police car if he could help it, nor go to the station. It was an aversion learned young. But his knees were sixty-eight years old now and still unfolding from the long flight. He must slip over to the Bier Schtube, somehow, to the nearest telephone, and call his lawyer. But how?

A curse bellowed from the root cellar. Kārlis glanced up in time to see a blue jumpsuit, climbing the stairs backwards with the stretcher, suddenly drop from view. Amid a splintering crash of wood, Kārlis heard the man scream. The stairs had collapsed.

The detective rushed to the root cellar and dropped to his knees beside the gaping hole. He waved an arm trying to clear rising dust. A ring of uniformed personnel pressed around him, peering down and shouting to one another.

Kārlis stared at their backs, heart drumming. This was his chance. This would be his only opportunity to get to a phone. Guts roiling, he strolled past the unmanned police cruiser. The radio squawked. The ambulance driver nodded to him. The linden tree, tired leafy sentry, leaned against the old house in a sloppy profusion of yellow flowers.

He'd made it around the side of the house, stepping through overgrown shrubs and tangled vines, without being stopped. Now headed into the forest, he walked faster. The Midsummer sky was bright as silver, illuminating an unused path Kārlis had once known like the back of his hand. After hiking for several minutes, he paused, turning his good ear toward the house. Blood pumped noisily in his head, drowning all sound. He pushed on, not hearing the running footsteps as much as otherwise sensing them. His heart nearly popped knowing that someone was overtaking him. Living in America, he'd forgotten how it felt to be afraid. There'd been a time here when he'd known the whole gamut of fear, ranging from constant dread to abject terror. It was all coming back.

K. Smiltens, 1945.

-1-

DECEMBER 21, 1940
BASTION HILL PARK
RIGA, LATVIA

KĀRLIS PĒRKONS DIDN'T TRUST ANYONE else to be the look-out. He had more to lose than the others, now that he'd been accepted to the Art Academy. He had more reason to avoid the secret police until at least graduation in June, besides the obvious fact that Stalin's henchmen, the NKVD, were vicious thugs. The problem was the fog. He parted the twigs of a frozen lilac bush and scouted below. A cloud pressed over the park like cotton packing the top of a pill bottle. Kārlis couldn't see, but he could hear his friends, buffooning around with the sled as if their lives depended on having some fun.

"It's just as dangerous to stay at home, you know."

"*Ak tu kungs!*" Kārlis nearly bit his tongue. Peters was right at his elbow. "Don't sneak up on me like that."

"Safer in the open," Peters contended, sweeping his arm across the hilltop view of the snow-clad park, its descending drifts and slopes, dim outlines of bare trees in the mist, and the suggestion of the distant Freedom Monument. "At home they know right where to find you. A bang at the door and whammo you're trapped." Peters flapped his arms like he was warming up for an Olympic event. "They come to my house, badgering my parents. I say stay on the move. Keep them guessing."

Kārlis removed his eyeglasses, steamed up by anxious breathing, and wiped the lenses with his wool glove. "But this could be an illegal assembly."

"What! Sledding?" Peters said.

"Well then where is everybody?" Kārlis said. "A year ago the whole senior class would've been horsing around in the snow."

The park was empty except for Eriks and Hugo dragging the sled up the hill, their every noise a deafening echo.

"*I threw flowers in the Gauja,*" belted out Eriks Gailis. He emerged from the white haze looking like a cross between a Viking raider and a trained bear. "*To send greetings to my girl.*"

"*Shhhh,*" Kārlis hissed. "I heard the folk songs are illegal."

"If his singing's been outlawed then there's a silver lining to this occupation," Peters said.

Eriks pushed the oak racer. It glided over hard packed snow to where Peters stopped it with a boot.

Peters and Eriks were about the same height, tall, and both loved besting the other. But Peters was the picture of fitness, the epitome of sportsmanship, whereas Eriks delighted in cheating. You never knew what he'd lummox into next.

"I was just telling Hugo here, the Communists are now organizing striptease performances," Eriks said, relishing the boys' attention. "All the party faithful went to the opening night at this cabaret in Riga, but after seeing the first show nobody went back. It was a huge flop and they had no idea why." With a mock-Russian accent, he said, "It vas superbly organized and all the strippers had solid Party records. They vere Bolsheviks from 1905!"

Peters chuckled and Hugo unleashed a silly, spasmodic laugh. No one cared whether the joke was even funny. They were starved for a good time, no matter how forced it felt.

"The bags were ancient," Hugo explained to Kārlis, mistaking his worried expression for idiocy. He cupped his hands under his breasts. "Shriveled elf shoes... in their fifties!"

"I get it," Kārlis said.

Hugo shrugged.

"Some of them even knew Lenin personally," Eriks added, wiping a tear from his eye.

"Ditch that bulky coat, Kārlis," Peters said, ever the competitor. "Mitigate degrees of wind resistance critical to peak sledding speed." He straddled the sled and maneuvered it to the hilltop's tipping point. "Let's show these turtles how it's done."

Kārlis played along. He made a show of removing his jacket and hanging it on a branch. He did it so he wouldn't lose his wallet in the snow. It held the card admitting him to the Art Academy, his ticket to the future.

Climbing on behind Peters, Kārlis crouched, bracing his feet against the runners, folding his knees like a cricket.

"Here lemme help," Eriks heckled. "I hope you like to eat snow!"

Kārlis felt the rascal push against his back, until the ground dropped away and the sled nosed downhill, chasing gravity to the bottom.

Freezing grits of snow nipped his cheeks.

"Yah ha!" Kārlis hooted, letting his guard down.

Then a runner caught, Peters yanked the steering bar and the sled jerked out of control, spraying a rooster tail of snow and spilling the boys over in a wipeout. Kārlis lay laughing so hard his guts shook.

Finally catching his breath, he adjusted his spectacles and rose on an elbow. He came nose-to-toe with a black boot.

A black, Russian boot.

Kārlis stopped laughing.

Wiping his face, he looked up.

The knee-high boot gave way to olive-green woolen breeches, which disappeared beneath a service coat cinched at the waist with a leather belt. The coat was buttoned to the neck, from where pointy collar tips aimed down at Kārlis. The man looming over him was old enough to be his father, but looked far sterner. He had big ears protruding beneath an officer's visor cap. The cap badge looked like a head wound, between the eyes, red under a gold hammer-and-sickle, the emblem of the NKVD.

His stomach churned. He was at the feet of the Communist secret police, the Cheka.

The big-eared officer said something in Russian that Kārlis didn't catch. The aggressive consonant clusters jackhammered his brain.

"I said, why aren't you in school?" the officer repeated, this time in Latvian.

Kārlis's throat clenched so he could barely breathe, let alone answer. Then he grasped that the officer wasn't addressing him, but Peters, who had rolled to a seated position in a nearby snow bank. Peters always attracted the attention of grownups, probably due to his athletically winning looks, strong jaw and assertive air. The coaches had always called Peters Leadership Material. Right now, Kārlis was glad to be the Poindexter-type that no one usually noticed.

"My classes are over for today," Peters said, rising slowly, brushing snow from his coat. "Comrade."

The officer clutched a handful of Peters's yellow hair and yanked him over.

"You go to high school, right?" he said, releasing Peters's head with a shove. "You're required to learn Russian."

"Yah, Comrade," Peters said. "Я учусь на русском, товарищ."

The language was alien, bewildering, and evil to Kārlis.

While Peters was trying to convince the officer that he *was* learning Russian, a dark-haired agent with sloping shoulders and swinging ape-arms was yelling and clomping up the hill. There was also a third man, standing behind the officer, younger, with a smooth, expressionless face, and a rifle butted against his shoulder pointed at the hilltop.

A *troika*; Kārlis had heard they worked in gangs of three. His stomach cramped at what else he'd heard.

"Come down with your hands up or I will shoot!" shouted the rifleman.

Kārlis was surprised, judging by his speech, the rifleman was a local, not one of the Russian occupiers. The rifle was pointed at a slender figure at the top of the hill, whom Kārlis knew was Hugo, peering down to see what was happening.

Kārlis held his breath, sensing Hugo's indecision.

Would his friend obey the authorities, or listen to the unseen Eriks on his other side, who was no doubt urging him to run. More likely Eriks had already fled the scene. Did Hugo even know, in this fog, that someone was aiming a gun at him?

Click.

Cocking the trigger cut the air sharply, commanded absolutely. Clear in any language.

Hugo obeyed. "Yah, okay," he said, picking a path down the slippery slope. "I'm coming."

Kārlis exhaled, relieved Hugo hadn't been shot, but at the same time wishing he'd gotten away.

"You have identification?" demanded the big-eared officer.

Peters reached into his coat. His hand was trembling when he took out his wallet and his school ID.

"Peters Kalnins," said the officer, squinting at the card. "I see you're *captain of the hockey team.*" His voice dripped with sarcasm. "You're a regular sport."

Peters's eyes flashed between the officer and the ID card, looking bewildered. Kārlis couldn't understand the mockery either. Adults usually praised Peters for being the best at everything.

"Who's your girlfriend?" the officer said, nodding toward Kārlis. "Let's see some ID."

Kārlis knew he could go to jail for not carrying ID at all times. He was just about to explain he'd left it on a tree when Hugo saved him by reaching over and presenting his student card.

The officer took it with a scowl, and compared Hugo to his photograph. Same willowy frame, silver-white hair, and ghostly-white skin, but the blue eyes were twice as big right now and brimming with tears.

"Hugo here is on the honor roll!" said the officer

with contempt. "What's your father do, boy?"

"He's a police officer. Was a police officer."

Kārlis held his breath, sensing that fact might get them in trouble. The Latvian police had been discharged from duty six months ago when the Soviets annexed the country.

"Uh-huh," said the big-eared officer. Then with a nod to his cohorts, he said, "That's enough. You maggots are coming with us."

Kārlis cursed silently. *Ak tu kungs!* They were screwed.

"We haven't done anything," Peters said.

"I doubt that," said the officer, sizing up the boys. "Student fraternity, church-going family, subversive reading material...you're guilty of something and I promise you'll confess it. Let's go."

The officer withdrew a club from his belt and gestured for them to move.

Something collapsed within Kārlis as huge hands grabbed him and shoved him down the trail out of the park. His heart pounded while details around him leapt into focus: fountains edged with icicles, statues of Latvian heroes, benches and shrubberies making odd, vague shapes under a thick blanket of snow. Crossing a bridge over the frozen canal that had once been the city's moat, they marched away from the stately Opera House, away from the spires and gabled rooftops of medieval Old Riga, toward the city's business district. The sled was left behind.

Kārlis felt he was on display as the NKVD paraded him down the slushy sidewalks of Freedom Boulevard, past the line-up of tall stone buildings. He prayed some adult would step up to help them, but shopkeepers and others disappeared into doorways and scurried elsewhere. He sensed the hidden audience watching him from behind shuttered windows and through the cracks of curtains.

"We didn't do anything," Peters said again, in a casual tone like he was trying to befriend the uniformed gorilla.

After a half dozen blocks, it became clear they were headed to the Corner House. The knowledge made Kārlis break out in sweat despite the freezing temperature. The NKVD headquarters was rumored to be a place of interrogation so ghastly no one spoke of it by its proper name. Instead they called it the Corner House, referring to its location at the intersection of Freedom and Stabu. *You go into the Corner House, you leave a corpse.* Peters knew it too, because when Kārlis met his eyes they were electric with terror.

Suddenly Peters stopped. He twisted around to face the agents surrounding him. "We'll answer your questions right here," he blurted. "Right now. What do you want to know?"

The tide sucking them toward the Corner House let up for a moment as the agents paused, staring curiously at Peters. Their red hammer-and-sickle cap badges glowed in the late afternoon light like monstrous, bloodshot eyes.

"Shut up," the rifleman said, resuming the march.

"Officer, you're Latvian," Peters said, appealing to the rifleman. "Please, just let us go home. I promise you'll never see us again."

This seemed to infuriate the man, the suggestion that he, as a Latvian, might be sentimental toward one of his own. To prove that he could be as nasty as any Russian, he pounced on Peters, poking him in the chest and neck with the barrel of his gun and backing him up the concrete steps leading to the door of the Corner House.

Article 58

Turning abruptly, Peters charged sideways into the ape-man, knocking him off balance. But the man recovered quickly, catching Peters and twisting his arm behind his back while Peters thrashed like a hooked bonefish.

The Cheka cursed furiously, manhandling Peters up the remaining stairs and pushing him toward the door.

At the last moment Peters kicked his legs forward with a scream. He braced one foot against each side of the doorjamb, refusing to cross the threshold and yelling, "We didn't do anything!"

Kārlis stood horrified. People were executed for resisting arrest, and that's what Peters was doing, two men could barely subdue him. It suddenly dawned on Kārlis, that only the old officer with the club was left to watch both Hugo and him.

Hugo must've had the same thought, because when Kārlis turned his head to look, Hugo was gone.

The old officer snapped his head around in time to see Hugo's back at the bottom of the concrete steps. He lunged after him with a vicious swing of his club, slipping and falling to the sidewalk.

Kārlis vaulted over the officer's splayed limbs, sliding and bumping hard down the stairs, impervious to pain. Using gloved hands like another set of feet, he righted himself and ran in the opposite direction as Hugo.

A whistle blew.

Kārlis didn't look back.

End of War, Going Home. K. Smiltens, 1945.

- 2 -

KĀRLIS RAN THROUGH A MAZE of city blocks until a
stitch in his side nearly paralyzed him. He ducked into a
recessed doorway, clutching his ribs. Trying not to gasp
conspicuously, he studied the boulevard. Daylight had
ebbed away. Yellow rectangles of light were appearing
in tall arrays on the buildings above. Commuters
with nervous, pinched faces were venturing out with
the shadows, hurrying to the rails, probably trying
to be tucked in somewhere safe before curfew. An
approaching trolley clanged, and an automobile nosed
its way down one side of the street. Contrary to what
he'd assumed, no one appeared to be chasing him,
nobody seemed aware of his crime or cared that he had
abandoned his friend at the NKVD torture chamber.
He wished someone did care. He felt like yelling,

*Hey everybody! They took my friend to the Corner House! A
good boy! He didn't do anything.*

Suddenly he was freezing. Since no one appeared to
be following him, he cut directly to the alley behind
Freedom Boulevard, and hurried home. It was an easy
walk. Most of the alley had been cleared of snow and

the back doors of the shops were as familiar to Kārlis as the storefronts. His father's leather workshop was on the next block. Papu would know what to do.

Slowing his pace, Kārlis approached warily. Some large-scale activity was underway in the alley, just outside Papu's loading dock. A sledge was parked there; harnessed to a mammoth Percheron blowing streams of white vapor from its nostrils and stamping giant hooves in the slush. At its head stood a man wearing a dusky blue fedora, fawn-colored gloves and a knee-length fur coat. The man held the animal's bridle near the bit, steadying the beast with strokes along its muscular neck.

This was probably someone picking up a shipment of leather goods, Kārlis surmised. Private commercial transactions were illegal as far as he knew, but Papu still engaged in the practice. Coming closer, Kārlis recognized the man as one of his father's associates.

"*Sveiks*, Mr. Zales," Kārlis said.

Zales and the horse both jerked as if Kārlis had run up flinging acid.

"Oh, it's only you, young Pērkons, er, Kārlis. I didn't see you coming," Zales said. He exhaled audibly, pressing his body against the horse's neck until the beast relaxed. "You mustn't call me Zales anymore, young man. I'm going by *Hill* now." He looked around furtively from under his fedora. "Everyone with the name Zales has been lined up and—" he dropped his voice, "well, executed. On account of there being parks and streets with the name."

"I'm sorry," was all Kārlis could think to say, wanting to cover his ears. He couldn't take in a grown man's problems right now, couldn't even absorb his own harrowing escape. "I had no idea, Mr. Zales."

"*Hill*, my boy, Hill. Distant cousins. Can't say I really

knew them. Nevertheless, can't be too careful. Don't underestimate Communist brutality."

Kārlis nodded at the warning, immediately applying it to what must be happening to Peters at the Corner House.

"I recommend you change your name as well," Zales said.

"Kārlis!" This was a high-pitched voice coming from the sledge. Kārlis was astonished to discover his little sister sitting up there, on the high-backed passenger bench amid a pile of furs.

"Biruta, what are you doing out after dark?" Kārlis said. "And in the alley to boot?"

"Did you know Papu is milking a cash cow?" Biruta said. Blonde braids tumbled from the hood of her cloak. On her lap she clutched a cardboard box poked with holes. "I want to know where he keeps the cow."

"What's going on here?" Kārlis said, perplexed to find his sister and her cat with Mr. Zales.

"I am escorting you to your summer house this evening," Zales said. "I owe your father a personal favor, you see. Great business instincts, your father has. Excellent sense of timing. If I hadn't listened to him, I'd be destitute, like everyone else in this city. Wake up one morning and *Poof.* Bank accounts drained. Everything over a thousand *lats* sucked away by the Politburo. Don't go up there," Zales said, seeing Kārlis about to enter the building. He dropped his voice, "There are Russians inside."

Kārlis froze mid-step. Russians. Here. *Ak tu kungs.* Had they come for him?

"Spies," Zales said in a loud whisper.

Kārlis processed the news, trying to reconcile it with the bumping and scraping he heard coming from the workshop. A moment later Kārlis's father emerged, dragging a trunk.

Janis Pērkons wore his usual fitted suit, vest and bowtie, spies and draft horses notwithstanding. He saw Kārlis and dropped the trunk.

"Ah! You made it!" his father said.

The next moment Kārlis was lifted off the ground in a bear hug, and held airborne. Suddenly, his eyes stung, his throat felt tight. He wiped his nose on his sleeve.

"Just in time," his father said, setting Kārlis back down.

"In time for what?"

"We're moving tonight," Janis said in a low voice. He nodded toward the upstairs family apartment. "Unexpected guests. A Soviet officer is here, wants to quarter a so-called apprentice with us. Someone to watch me at work. Probably my replacement." His father balled a fist, and looked like he wanted to throw it through the brick wall. "He's planning to sleep in the hallway outside my bedroom."

"You should abandon this operation now," Zales interjected, still holding the horse. "Before they drop the ax."

"Moving?" Kārlis said, suddenly grasping the meaning of the loaded sledge. "When are we coming back?"

Instead of answering, his father hoisted the trunk onto the sledge, lodging it firmly between other crates. Pushing off his fur-lined cap, steam rose from the top of his shaved head.

"So they haven't come for me?" Kārlis said.

"Why would they come for *you?*" his father asked, turning sharp blue eyes to him. His father's moustache and goatee were always precisely trimmed, exuding the comforting notion that Janis

Pērkons was working a plan.

"Because they caught me sledding and took me to the Corner House," Kārlis said, the words pouring out in a panic.

His father listened to the details with a cold stare, giving vent to an oath.

"I barely got away," Kārlis concluded. "But they took Peters in there and we've got to get him out."

Janis exchanged a look with Zales, and by the time he faced Kārlis again, a hardness had set around his eyes. "Son, I know you want to hear me say that I can fix this," he said. "That I know someone or some way."

That was exactly what Kārlis wanted to hear. Everyone knew Janis Pērkons was a problem solver, a big-thinker, a man with connections.

"But I don't!" His father pulled out his cigarettes and Mr. Zales stepped forward to light him up. "I have your mother and sister to think about, too."

Kārlis said nothing while Janis blew smoke toward heaven, still certain his father had a brilliant solution up his sleeve.

"You know what they do to people there," Kārlis finally said, his voice cracking. "That could be me dragged in there."

Janis looked like Kārlis had slapped him.

Mr. Zales ran his arm over the horse's neck.

An impatient *meow* came through the holes in Biruta's box.

Finally, his father said, "Son, do you understand the principle of triage?"

No, and Kārlis wasn't in the mood for a French lesson.

His father took the tone of a sympathetic philosopher. "On a battlefield, medics separate the wounded into three groups. Those who are not seriously injured;

those who are seriously injured but may be saved; and those who are too far gone—"

"That's garbage," Kārlis blurted, eyes bulging. "I'm not listening to that. If it was me in the Corner House right now, would I be *too far gone?*"

"Thank God it's not you," his father said with a steely edge. "Because there still would not be a goddam thing I could do, but so help me I would put up everything trying to save you."

Kārlis didn't know where to look or how to stand, his world suddenly foreign.

"The fact is, you escaped, for now," Janis said, taking a last drag and throwing his cigarette down. "God help me for rejoicing in that." He looked Kārlis in the eye and clapped his shoulders. "Look, son. I didn't expect to be moving tonight, but a Soviet squatter is here to watch us. I won't have him making himself at home with your mother and Biruta. And you should stay as far away from this so-called apprentice as possible. He's trouble. That's why I'm taking the family to the country right away. I wish you'd go with them."

The box *meowed* again.

Kārlis felt hopelessly flat. He'd been clutching at the string of his father's balloon, only to find that without the lift of Papu's will, he was left holding a damp, heavy heap of nothing. His father was not going to step up and make things right. Kārlis didn't want to cry in front of the men, so he shifted to the offensive. "Why aren't *you* going with them?"

"I have a business to run," Janis said, returning to the job of packing the sledge. "I'll commute on the train as often as possible."

"Well, I have to go to school," Kārlis said, his voice husky. "I have to pass classes to graduate. I have to graduate to attend the Art Academy." *His ticket to the future.*

"I understand how important that is to you," Janis said. He was securing the load with a leather strap, tugging with unnecessary force. "But if the NKVD has your name, they can easily pick you up at school. Or arrest you here at the Leather Works. Might be better for you to come out to the country for now. Maybe when the situation's less volatile you can go back to studying art."

Kārlis didn't like the sound of that, but he didn't know what to do. He'd thought he'd escaped the NKVD running through the streets, not knowing they were already in his home, moving in while his family was moving out. If they wanted to, they could track him down. There was no getting away from them. But that didn't mean he should just hide in the country with his mother.

"I think I should keep going to classes," Kārlis said. "The Cheka didn't even get my name."

"Son, they will get your name from Peters," Janis said darkly. "If they want it."

Kārlis's stomach curdled. People kept saying things that sent him down the dark corridors of the Corner House to where the Cheka did unspeakable things to Peters. He stared at the sledge.

"They're not that systematic, thank God," Mr. Zales said, weighing in with his two centimes. "But what they lack in organization, they make up for with an unfathomable cruel streak."

The tap of footsteps made them look toward the workshop, from where Kārlis's mother emerged, slipping on the hood of her travelling cloak. She hadn't taken time to tidy her hair, a brown strand seemed plastered to a wet cheek. Her eyes and nose were red. Seeing his mother upset always made Kārlis feel terrible, even when it wasn't his fault.

At a glance, she said, "Have you lost your coat?"

Kārlis folded his arms over his thermal undershirt. Now that she mentioned it, he was freezing.

His father helped his mother up the running board to her seat on the sledge.

"Climb up here before you freeze," she said to Kārlis. "Come on, get under the rugs."

Kārlis's thinking felt numb and slow, but he knew he didn't feel right warming up under the furs with his mother and sister. "I'm not ready to leave yet, Mother," he said. "I just—I have school and some things to straighten out. You know, about being accepted to the Art Academy. But I'll come as soon as I can."

"But I've packed your things," Mother said. "Janis, what's wrong with him? Make him come."

"He knows how to find his way home, Anna. He's nearly eighteen," Janis said. "Let him find his sea legs. That way is safer in the long run."

His mother looked unconvinced but before she could argue, Janis said, "Son, if you insist on staying in Riga, vary your routine. Don't be predictable."

"Changing addresses has become the national hobby," Zales said.

"I have places to stay," Kārlis said.

"Don't trust anybody," Janis said.

"Let's get cracking," Zales said. "Curfew sneaks up quick."

"Here, put this blanket around you," his mother said, handing down a velvety-thing with long, silky gold fringe.

Janis held the horse's head while Zales climbed up on the driver's bench. "I just realized tomorrow's the solstice," Zales said, organizing the reins and hunkering into his fur coat. "The darkest day of the year."

18

Janis released the harness and walked to the horse's rump. Looking up at Zales, he said quietly, "Rudolfs, if anything happens to me, promise you'll help Anna and the children."

Kārlis felt he shouldn't have heard that and wanted to cover his ears.

"Of course I will," Zales said. "But dammit Janis, stop taking unnecessary risks. These black market deals are foolhardy. They've noticed you." Zales tipped his head upward, presumably to where the Russians sat around Mother's dining table having tea.

"I have no choice," Janis said. "Surviving this will require reserves. The deeper the better. They'll eventually get around to taking the Leather Works. And then it's going to be dry for a long time."

Janis stepped on the running board and leaned over boxes and duffels to kiss the passengers, saying "Goodbye, Cookie. Take good care of Katkis. Anna, I'll see you soon."

"*Sveiks*, Papu," Biruta said.

The horse moved out energetically, as if also eager to beat curfew. Starting with a lurch, the sledge then glided smoothly. Biruta flipped around in her seat. Rising to her knees, she poked her head over the seat back and held up a small hand.

Kārlis waved back, following the sledge down the alley for a few steps, the reality of their leaving sinking in with an empty chill.

Turning back to the Leather Works, Kārlis sucked in his breath and froze. Someone had crept up and was lurking in the doorway directly behind his father, silhouetted by the light of the workshop. Whoever he was, he also watched the sledge depart, with a vacuous expression that made Kārlis's skin crawl.

His father was holding his pocket watch up to the dim window light. "They should be there by nine," he

19

said, snapping the cover closed and sliding the watch into his vest pocket. He must have read the alarm in Kārlis's eyes, because when he turned to go inside he didn't act surprised to see the guy standing there.

"Igor Volkov, my worthy apprentice," Janis said, smoothly.

Igor Volkov didn't return the greeting. He was looking around the workshop and at the departing sledge, as if he'd caught Kārlis and his father pilfering supplies. Kārlis immediately resented the Russian, who was around his own age, for acting like he had some sort of authority over them in their own family business.

Volkov had a heart-shaped face with vigorous red circles on high cheekbones. A wave of brown hair dipped over his forehead. His lips were perfectly symmetrical. Kārlis would've called it a pretty-boy face, were it not for the haughty eyes of stone and the muscled upper body that made Kārlis feel like a bespectacled idiot wrapped in his mother's blanket.

Janis spoke like everything was business as usual. "It's time to give the immersion drums a final rotation and close shop for the day," he said. "Give me a hand with these doors, Igor, will you?" Janis grasped one side of the steel door and began dragging it, screeching, on its rollers.

The apprentice ignored Janis, staring acidly at Kārlis.

His father hadn't introduced him as his son or even acknowledged Kārlis's presence. Janis Pērkons held a reputation for gallantry, so Kārlis understood the slight was deliberate, probably an attempt to shield him from this nasty Russian infiltrator. Still Kārlis felt somewhat disinherited.

"Grab the door," Janis repeated, pointing to the handle near Igor Volkov.

"Comrade. I came out because I need a key to this place," Igor said, declining to help.

"Yah, of course," Janis said. He made a show of patting his pockets before turning to Kārlis and saying, "Do you happen to have a key on you?" Then he went to close the other side of the door himself.

Kārlis was stupefied. On top of everything else, his father now intended to give this interloper his key?

Kārlis extracted his keys, which were on a fob of leather and amber he'd crafted in this very workshop. He pried the key off wondering what next? This *kāpost galva* freeloader would be bunking in his room among his clipper ship models and books and sketches?

Janis had, by now, closed the workshop doors by all but a few inches, through which Kārlis passed the key. Janis took it and tossed it to Volkov, giving Kārlis a nod. It was a portentous nod, a compendium of fatherly advice and concern.

Volkov snatched the key midair. Through the narrow crack between doors, Kārlis saw Igor Volkov smile and was reminded of a wolf baring its teeth.

Then his father shut the doors with a clang, and Kārlis was standing alone in the freezing alley.

Night Crawlers, K. Smiltens. 1945

- 3 -

THERE WAS NO QUESTION WHERE to go next. Kārlis flew down the alley like a homing pigeon. After fifteen minutes he'd reached the Leopolds family bakery at 24 Freedom Boulevard, where he'd find Jekabs Leopolds, one of his best friends. Checking both directions to be sure no one was watching, he barged through the back door to the kitchen.

Mixing bowls clattered as the baker turned sharply. "Oy! Kārlis!"

"Sorry to frighten you, Mr. Leopolds."

Mr. Leopolds exhaled heavily and crossed the room. "Been a little jumpy lately, that's all. Get over here, boychik," he said, pulling Kārlis close and thumping his back, which was a minor beating because the baker was very muscular from pummeling dough all day. "You made it." Apparently he'd heard about the Corner House. "Thank the Lord."

"Yah," Kārlis said, "I made it." *Peters didn't make it. I was supposed to be the look-out.* Kārlis kept his face in a frozen mask, but eventually the tingle of a thaw crept over him. Not only had he escaped the NKVD today but, for the first time in his life, he'd taken a course independent from his parents. He felt vaguely uneasy as he warmed up in the brightly lit kitchen, suddenly wishing his family were with him. This haven, with its soothing aroma of fresh bread, contrasted miserably with the memory of his mother and sister leaving home, and his father shutting him out in a dark alley with the parting advice, *don't trust anybody.*

"Look who's here, Hugo," Mr. Leopolds said to a slumped figure sitting near the ovens. "One more buddy you can stop worrying about."

Kārlis nodded at Hugo, relieved to see he'd also gotten away.

Against the blackened brick, Hugo's face and hair were shock-white. He met Kārlis with red, swollen eyes. Then he returned his gaze to the embers, watching them with a dazed expression, until his face was jerked by some hiccupping twitch.

"Did you tell anyone you were coming here?" Mr. Leopolds asked Kārlis, cracking the back door and surveilling the alley.

"No," Kārlis said, disgruntled that Mr. Leopolds even had to ask.

The baker closed the door, grabbed a log off the firewood stack and stoked one of the ovens, fanning with the bellows until flames erupted. Dusting off his hands, he went back to the mixing bowls, kneading a large blob of dough with the fervor of one man strangling another. Stopping suddenly, Mr. Leopolds straightened his yarmulke with the back of his fist, and said. "Any news about Peters?"

"No," Kārlis said, feeling shame heat his cheeks.

"A terrible thing," Mr. Leopolds said, shaking his head. "God forbid! It shouldn't happen. You look beat. Want a roll? Cup of coffee?"

"No, thank you, Mr. Leopolds. I'm not hungry."

"Well, my nephew's back there, with the usuals," Mr. Leopolds said, pointing toward the pantry. "Tell them to keep it down, would you? Juveniles need a place to blow off a little steam, make some sense of things. That I know," he said, wiping his brow, "but six of you in one place—whew! We're in trouble if we're caught." He worked the dough with a grim set to his jaw. "Still, you can't just cave," he muttered. "A miserable year."

"I'll tell them to keep it down," Kārlis said, proceeding to the pantry. Hugo got up and followed him.

The pantry was a large, windowless room lit by a bare bulb hanging from the ceiling. Exclusive as a clubhouse and chummy as a locker room, it was stacked with 50-kilo bags of flour that had been positioned like furniture. Turning the doorknob triggered a subtle change in the room's pulse, as if the cronies inside had all shifted slightly to form some desired tableau. They were hiding something, Kārlis thought, maybe just the fact that they'd been crying.

Jekabs reclined in the corner, a cigarette between his lips, nose in a textbook.

Standing over him was Sniedze, who jerked his head up, saucer-eyed.

Vilz appeared to be reorganizing pans on a shelf.

Eriks sat slumped in the chair, which he'd lowered from its tipped position.

After Kārlis walked in and Hugo closed the door behind them, there was a nearly imperceptible, collective exhale.

"It's just Kārlis," Jekabs said, by way of greeting.

With a moan, Vilz shoved the nest of pans aside revealing, to Kārlis's dismay, the hiding place of her portable typewriter.

Eriks lifted a flask from behind his tree-trunk of a thigh, tipped the chair again and took a swig.

Jekabs sat up, fanned the pages of the textbook he was supposedly reading, to where he'd slipped a scrap of paper. "Where were we?" he asked, standing to look over Vilz's shoulder.

Vilz read from the sheet in the typewriter, "Among them were Lukins Nikolajs, police officer; Guntis Kesteris, clergyman..."

"Right," Jekabs said, referring to his scrap. "So, what? We just add Peters's name to the bottom of the list?" He wiped his nose on his sleeve.

"Yah," Vilz said, clacking at the steel keys, "Peters Kalnins, student."

"What's that?" Kārlis asked.

Vilz held her hand out and Jekabs passed her the cigarette.

"List of people arrested for counterrevolutionary activity yesterday and today," Vilz said. She blew a stream of smoke at the light bulb. "I happened to be writing it up for *Free Latvia*." She nodded at the typewritten sheet. "Thought it'd be just another list of names and crimes. Then Eriks careened in, told us what happened at the park. Suddenly it's personal. We got Peters on that list now." Vilz pushed her lips together grimly, making dimples appear in her cheeks.

"Counterrevolutionary activity?" Kārlis said. "We were sledding."

Kārlis looked up to Vilz Zarins, who, at eighteen, was the oldest of the friends. Vilz brought a worldly air to the pantry since she regularly attended "secret meetings". She wore her dark hair in a short wave barely covering a creamy neck, and parted decisively down the middle, framing agate-blue eyes. Curves shifted under her long-sleeved thermal when she positioned the Adler toward the light to read what she had typed.

26

Article 58

"Offenses include being a wealthy farmer, a capitalist businessman, member of a student organization, decorated with the Oak Leaf military order, criticizing the Communist Party, hiding in the forest, not singing at a labor rally, and, oh, the one you boys know so well," Vilz added pointedly, "illegal assembly and singing a folk song."

Kārlis squirmed.

Eriks tipped the flask up, a grim twist to his mouth. "Kārlis was supposed to be the *kāpost galva* look-out."

"It was your idea to go in the first place," Kārlis said. "And your singing like a buffoon that brought the Cheka down. Then you get away without even being seen."

"The entire episode was disgraceful and demoralizing." Hugo interjected, sounding like one of their teachers.

Clack, clack, clack, clack. Vilz was back to typing.

"Is it true you two left Peters to fight NKVD agents alone?" Eriks said.

"What's the point in casting blame?" Vilz said loudly from behind her typewriter.

"You were not even there," Kārlis told Eriks. "So just shut up." Then something caught his eye. "What in hell is that? Are you actually wearing a boutonniere? What, are you going dancing tonight?"

"Now my button hole bothers you?"

"What bothers me is that at some point during the last hour while I was running for my life, you were pinning a sprig of holly to your lapel."

"When we argue among ourselves, it works out great for the Commies," Vilz said.

Kārlis took a deep breath and closed his mouth, deciding to drop it. Shaking his head, he took off his gloves one by one and pelted them at the corner.

"Can't change what happened," Vilz said, without looking up from the typewriter. "Can only do it different going forward."

"What do you think they're doing to Peters right now?" Hugo said in a croaky voice.

The burning question hung there, sucking air from the room.

Kārlis dropped his eyes to the baseboard. He tried not to think about the slow ripping of fingernails, temple screws and things that shouldn't even be done to animals. "We ought to be talking about getting him out of there," he said. "Hugo, can't your father do something? Doesn't he know someone from his police force days?"

"My dad's in no position to stick his neck out," Hugo said. "We don't even have a place to live anymore."

"What about the League of Nations?" Kārlis persisted. "Latvia's a member, doesn't that count for anything?"

"No. Nobody cares," Vilz said. *Clack, clack, clack.* "The world only cares that Nazis have overrun Paris. Nobody's going to help us, but us." She tugged the paper off the roller with a zip, faced the others, and said quietly, "In the next edition of *Free Latvia* I'm going to inform people about what happened." She gave the article to Kārlis. "As my tribute to Peters. Everybody will know what those red *kāpost galvas* have done."

"You don't have to talk about Peters like he's dead," Kārlis said, swallowing dryly. Something told him he should leave now. Anything concerning *Free Latvia* was dangerous. But there was no place else to go. So, adjusting his glasses, he scanned the draft newsletter of the resistance.

Article 58

Seeing Peters named with those who'd been rounded up by the NKVD made Kārlis feel like he was in someone else's body. He wiped his nose on his sleeve. Then he read the next line, and his eyes blasted out of his head.

"All arrested received the *death penalty* and were *executed* according to authority granted under Article 58 of the Russian Criminal Code!"

The room turned upside down.

"What is this?" Kārlis said. "You've already decided among yourselves that Peters has— what? Been executed?"

"Or will have been by the time this goes to press," Vilz said, latching the cover to her typewriter and returning it to its hiding place.

"I don't buy it," Kārlis said, looking around at the others. "We were just with him."

He looked to Hugo for backup but only saw a look of doom carved in the salt-white face.

"You go into the Corner House, you come out a corpse," Sniedze parroted.

"No," Kārlis said, thinly. "That's just something people say."

Eriks lowered the chair to the floor and got up. He handed Kārlis the flask like it was an olive branch. "Sorry I jumped all over you," he said. "It wasn't your fault."

Somehow Eriks's humility made Kārlis feel even worse, but he took the flask.

"I brought your coat," Eriks said, tugging the fringy blanket.

Kārlis had forgotten it was draped around his shoulders. Maybe Eriks wasn't such a selfish clod after all, he thought, as a belt of vodka burned nastily down his throat. He went to the coat hook and checked his pockets. His wallet was still there, including the card admitting him to the Art Academy. Seeing his name engraved there made his heart flutter with relief. Maybe his entire future hadn't been flushed down the NKVD toilet today after all.

"I'm sorry to break it to you like this, Kārlis," Vilz said. "I know how you like to hide your head in the sand."

Kārlis ignored that. Vilz criticized anyone who didn't go to her secret meetings. "I just...I don't agree to admitting Peters is dead," Kārlis said.

"Pray to God he is," Vilz said.

These oblique nods to torture were getting under Kārlis's skin.

Sniedze Krasts pushed his way to the center of the pantry, blurting, "At least if he's dead, he won't be able to give our names to the Cheka." Sniedze Krasts, dwarfed by the oversized newsboy cap he always wore, was the runt of the gang, and a dimwit as far as Kārlis was concerned. His freckles looked weirdly prominent against a sickly complexion. "But if he's *not* dead, we should change our names, just in case, so the Ivans can't find us. You can disguise being Latvian by dropping the *-s* or *-is* off your name. You'd just be Karl," Sniedze said to Kārlis.

"Why would I want to Germanize my name?" Kārlis said, hoping he sounded aloof and scornful. His heart raced at the notion the Cheka might hunt him down.

"To disguise it so you don't match the name on the list," Sniedze said.

"What list?" Jekabs said.

"I'm keeping my name," said Vilz who, even when Kārlis first met her in nursery school, had always insisted on being called a variation of her father's name, refusing her given, pink ruffle of a name, Virma.

"What list?" Jekabs repeated.

"They put your name on a list before they come get you," Sniedze said. "My neighbor, Mr. Ozols, told me."

"There you go! See what I'm saying?" Jekabs said, smacking Sniedze upside the head. Jekabs could do that without being mean. There was something steadying about his no-nonsense practicality. "You talk like some eavesdropping, name-dropping schlub!"

"You are never to even utter my name," Kārlis told Sniedze. "Don't even let on that you know me."

"Seriously, stop it with the blabbing, Sniedze," Eriks said.

"Get some discretion," Hugo said.

"We ought to make aliases so we don't match the names on the list is all I'm saying," Sniedze continued, spitting defensively. "And maybe disguises, too. Stalin changed *his* name. From Ioseb Besarionis to Man of Steel. Guess what he did when his doctor told him he was clinically paranoid? Killed him! Then he killed a hundred thousand other doctors so no one could ever call him a madman again. *A hundred thousand. God*, I can't even picture that many medical professionals. Rubbing the six of us out would be nothing to him. Oh, what if Peters gives them our names?"

"Just stop talking gibberish for a minute, would you?" Jekabs said.

"Yah, let's get organized," Vilz said, using the calm, confiding tone that had lured a number of students to her underground meetings. "This is what we do."

Kārlis had to admit, it was comforting to let Vilz take charge.

"First off, we'll publish this," Vilz said, holding up her freshly typewritten page. "Along with the article about the legs poking out of the ground in the forest."

Kārlis nodded. So far it didn't sound too hard.

"I type the articles. Kārlis gives me some illustrations. Eriks, I need a brute like you to keep watch while Jekabs and me work the printing press. When the printing's done, everybody will distribute the flyers. Get them in the hands of readers *without getting caught*."

Jekabs nodded, fists on hips.

"Distribute the flyers without getting caught," Eriks repeated, eyebrows raised. It sounded more dangerous when Eriks said it.

"Yah. Don't be obvious about it," Vilz said. "Don't look like you're hiding anything either. Just *nonchalantly* drop copies here and there, under doors, in market baskets. Leave a couple around school and in the park and wherever you go."

"Nonchalantly drop copies here and there," Eriks repeated.

A nest of metal hit the floor with a clang that made everybody jump. Sniedze had somehow fallen, knocking pans off the shelf with a fumbling that would've been comic if it hadn't given Kārlis a heart attack.

"Like that for example," Eriks said, dryly. "Nonchalant like Sniedze." Everyone cracked up watching the nitwit try and fail to regain his balance, wobbling amongst the ringing bowls. It felt good to laugh, releasing the panic that had been tamped down and corked up all day.

Jekabs balanced a round pan on an upraised finger and set it twirling above beefy, flour-dusted forearms. "This is the way a Nonchalant does it," he said. He used the word *Nonchalant* like it was a title of respect, a moniker for specially inducted members to an elite society. "Notice the poise, the finesse."

"Right," said Vilz, going along with the play, "and a Nonchalant delivering flyers is a stealthy *kāpost galva*."

"A Nonchalant wears a sharp crease in his fedora," Kārlis said. "That's the look we want."

"Yah, and those black-faced watches you guys have. That's a sign of a Nonchalant."

"And English newspapers."

Everyone seemed pleased at the name. Each tenet of a Nonchalant was voted in with the tip and pass of the flask. The camaraderie made Kārlis feel braver, even somewhat invincible. By God, together they would do something about Peters and their doomed futures. Nobody else would. He'd acclimated already to the danger of the plan.

"A Nonchalant will never be bullied into hiding his Latvian name," someone quipped.

"Never abandon another Nonchalant."

"Never divulge Nonchalant secrets to an outsider."

Kārlis felt competitive and a little tipsy. No one wanted to be the next dolt in line who couldn't add to the code.

"A Nonchalant will never lie to another Nonchalant," one said.

"Or steal his girl."

"Or give up the names of our members, no matter what they do to you."

"We will valiantly defend a fellow Nonchalant."

Vilz was buoyant at the show of solidarity. "This is an auspicious beginning," she said. "Knowing we can trust each other."

Don't trust anyone. Papu's advice echoed unpleasantly in the chambers of Kārlis's memory. He ignored it, driving the Nonchalant vows like a stake into his heart.

"So, everybody's in," Vilz said, looking around the circle. "We are six intrepid Nonchalants!"

"Seven," Hugo said thickly, jutting out his jaw. "Peters. He went down fighting, I'm so proud of him."

"Yah. Peters is one of us."

"He's the chief Nonchalant."

"The epitome of how a Nonchalant should be, Peters."

"Eriks? You look doubtful," Vilz said. "You're in, right?"

Eriks seemed to be staring at something on the other side of the wall, as if the thought he wished to express lurked over there. Finally he said, "Seems to me anyone caught with a copy of your rag is dead meat. If I'm going to risk my neck, I'd rather do it for something that counted, not passing notes."

"I'm listening," Vilz said.

Eriks was breathing loudly.

"Let's torch the goddam Corner House. That hellhole of Commie sadism has got to be put down."

The silly one-liners dried up at once. Kārlis swallowed hard, realizing he'd graduated to swimming in the deep end. He was aware of his own breathing, of the thinness of the pantry walls, and of too much booze buzzing past his ears. He noticed the others had also been jolted by this thunderclap proposition. They seemed to proceed with carefully chosen words.

"And just how would you go about doing that?" asked Jekabs.

"With explosives," Eriks said. "Dynamite. A bomb."

"Not going to be able to get our hands on one of those," Jekabs said.

"At a minimum, we'd need some kind of accelerant," Hugo said. He seemed to be embracing the logistical challenges of arson as a welcome escape from the day's unfathomable emotional crisis. This might be a problem he could actually solve.

"Blow that torture pit to smithereens," Eriks said darkly.

"More likely we could interrupt its operations for an interval," Hugo said.

Vilz's eyes lit up. "Have you heard of a Molotov?"

"Russian Secretary of State," Hugo replied.

"Not the politician," Vilz said. "There's a very cheap, but potent little firebomb named after him. Easy to make. Finns put it to good use last year."

"Something we could concoct ourselves?"

"We just need bottles, rags and some petrol. I think high-proof Vodka would work," Vilz said. "Then we just *nonchalantly* drop a few of those babies in the basement window of the Corner House."

"I like it," Eriks said.

"Lob a few upstairs."

"Yah. All Nonchalant-like."

"That would start something burning. Be hell to put out. Incinerate those devils in their own cage."

"How's that gonna help Peters?" Kārlis said. "What if he's trapped there?"

"Too late to help Peters," Vilz said. "But we can help the next fellow, in Peters's name."

It seemed disloyal to point out any flaws in the proposal. It was now a matter of Nonchalant pride to execute the plan. Otherwise the code of behavior they'd just touted would be exposed as empty words, Peters's tribute mere lip service.

Kārlis felt the sharp horns of dilemma goring him in every direction: dangerous to go down this path, unsafe not to. He drained the flask when it came around. The scheme *could* work. With Eriks's nerve, Hugo's brains, Vilz's connections, Jekabs's practical good sense, and Sniedze staying the hell away, they might get away with such mischief.

"We got the rags," Eriks said, lifting Kārlis's fringed blanket. "Bet we can swipe a case of empty bottles from the alley."

"Where we gonna get that much vodka?"

The ensuing silence was worrisome, threatening to slow their momentum.

"Would denatured alcohol work?" Kārlis asked.

"Yah," said Hugo.

"Well," Kārlis said, "We could *nonchalantly* pick some up at my father's workshop."

Sniedze giggled.

"How soon could we get that?" Vilz asked.

Shrugging, Kārlis said, "No time like the present."

"I'll roll with your idea, because I'm glad you're finally doing something," Vilz said, "not because I think it's better than publishing the truth." She held up her typed page. "One newspaper is worth a thousand firebombs."

Vilz proceeded to lay out the plan. Tonight, Kārlis, Eriks and Sniedze would procure the necessary materials. Vilz, Jekabs and Hugo would print the newsletters, any risk in that having been upstaged by the sabotage plot. They would all meet the next day to assemble what Vilz called Molotov Cocktails. Then they'd roast NKVD for dinner.

The pantry door shot open like a cattle prod to Kārlis's ribs and Mr. Leopolds walked in. Kārlis caught his breath and tried to look natural. Mr. Leopolds was about to grab a can of shortening when he stopped. He plucked the empty flask off the shelf and sniffed the pour spout. Putting his hand on his hip, his eyes took in the circle of them.

"Oy, this makes me very nervous," Mr. Leopolds said, wagging the flask. "You kids, I understand how difficult it is to work through what's happening." He shook his head. "When I was your age I was, well, idealistic. It's a shock to learn that the world is not just." He looked at the flask, seeming frustrated that he couldn't find the words he wanted.

Kārlis liked Mr. Leopolds. He felt bad for plotting revolution on his premises and deceiving him about it. There would be consequences if they were caught. Mr. Leopolds was not a schnook, a word Kārlis had learned from the baker.

"But you have got to understand you cannot be caught drinking, you cannot put one toe out of line!" Mr. Leopolds said. "As it is, this is an illegal assembly. You can't even give the impression you're in some club or fraternity. You'll never understand how a Russian thinks. For that matter, you can't trust anybody."

"Don't worry, Uncle Eli," Jekabs said. "We won't."

"I just think you boys—and Vilz—all of us—should get a good night's sleep. Things will look better in the morning."

Kārlis looked at the ground. He heard Eriks say, "We were just going, Mr. Leopolds."

"Don't be seen leaving here all at once," Mr. Leopolds said, as everybody gathered their coats and filed out. "This is a bad situation, that I know. If you kids are having trouble handling this, come back in the morning. Let's have a cup of coffee and talk about it. But until then, well," Mr. Leopolds tapped the flask reproachfully, "promise me you won't do anything reckless."

Street Urchins. K. Smiltens, 1945.

- 4 -

ELBOW TO ELBOW WITH ERIKS and Sniedze, Kārlis marched along Freedom Boulevard, the wind sinking its teeth into his throat. Already less euphoric about stealing alcohol from his father's leather workshop, he regretted leaving the toasty cocoon of the bakery. He was thinking longingly of coffee and bread when Eriks nudged him in the ribs. A trio of men had come around the corner up ahead across the street. Without needing to see more, Kārlis felt an overpowering urge to turn tail and run. That strategy had already saved him from the clutches of the Corner House. But he stayed in lockstep with Eriks and Sniedze. If he ran, they would all have to run. He pulled his fedora lower and clutched his collar, hoping the men would go about their business and let them pass.

As they drew closer, Kārlis could see the uniforms were not NKVD green. The men had no insidious red cap badges or weapons. They looked like city maintenance workers. In fact, they were painters. One dragged a ladder, another carried buckets, and the third man dripped paint from a long handled roller. Their monotonous painter chatter faded as the boys reached the corner and turned in unison, with the tight precision of three minnows trying to give the impression they were a bigger fish.

Just when Kārlis remembered to breathe, believing he'd gotten away, Eriks nudged him again. Without taking his hand from his coat pocket, Eriks pointed up to the cloisonné street sign embedded in the building's masonry. Freedom had been changed to Lenin. Grey paint dripped down the stones, the white letters were still shiny wet.

"Whew! That was a close one," Sniedze said, in a thin voice. "But they're just changing the name. Just paint."

Kārlis balled up his fists. "Shut up," he muttered. It was more than just paint.

They ducked into the alley and ran the rest of the way to Pērkons Leather Works. The premises were in pitch black. Kārlis had given up his key, so he intended to enter through the second floor window that his mother always left open a crack. As he studied the target window, snow slid off the nearby eaves landing in the alley with a plop. Jamming his toes in the grout cracks, Kārlis grasped the easy handholds of the rough masonry and scaled the building like a cat. At the second floor, he grabbed the concrete curls of a stone face and balanced his knee on the sill. The window slid open smoothly and he climbed inside, straightening up at one end of a hallway that stretched the length of the apartment.

Down in the alley, Eriks and Sniedze were watching him with craned necks. Kārlis gave them a nod and slid the glass closed noiselessly. Turning to the dark apartment, he watched and listened for the Russian punk who'd been assigned to the Leather Works, supposedly as an apprentice. He passed his mother's tapestries and bookshelves, his sister's collection of folkloric dolls, sensing on them the stench of foreign occupation fondling. Loath to confront the apprentice-spy, he slinked over to the tight wooden stairway that went directly to the workshop and descended, expertly dodging the creaky boards.

It was eerie, being alone in the high-ceilinged workshop where a crew of tradesmen usually hustled to fill his father's orders. Dim light fell on the shop floor making towering stacks of hides cast a gathering of shaggy-monster shadows around the large central cutting surface. Workbenches with dyes and blades, innocently lined up in neat rows by day, now looked weirdly ominous. Kārlis swallowed, grounding himself in the familiar aromas of saddle soap and tobacco. He'd take the denatured alcohol from the cupboard across the room, where massive rotating immersion drums chugged rhythmically as though the workday hadn't ended. It would be a simple errand, he reminded himself.

Then a murmur reached Kārlis's ear making the hair on the back of his neck rise. He looked up to his father's loft-level office where light seeped through cracks in the shutters. Had his father forgotten to turn off the radio? No. Men were up there, behind the closed door speaking in low tones. Kārlis instantly changed his plan, needing to know Papu was okay. He crept along the wall where stairs rose to the loft. At the top he pressed against the office door, listening.

"What is your decision, Mr. Pērkons?"

One of the window slats had closed crookedly, allowing a narrow view to the interior.

Half expecting his father to be hosting an illicit card game, Kārlis gasped at what he saw instead. The desk lamp illuminated Janis Pērkons, still in his bowtie and vest with rolled-up shirtsleeves, bending over a glittering pile of treasure. Lengths of gold chain lay serpentine on the desk amid coins and chunks of molten gold, a yellow heap flecked with jewels. With a jeweler's loupe pressed to his eye, Janis held a tiara to the lamp, scrutinizing diamonds set in the filigree that scattered a brilliant spectral refraction around the tiny triangle of the room visible to Kārlis.

His father shifted behind the desk, suggesting he faced at least two unseen men, black market operators, Kārlis assumed, waiting his decision.

Kārlis held his breath. He wanted to back away unseen, but was suddenly too afraid to move in any direction.

His father, however, set down the tiara unhurriedly. He picked up a gold chain at least two meters long and stretched a section of it against the light, assessing and calculating with a practiced eye.

A set of vulture-like shoulders lurched into the frame, belonging to someone who fingered a brooch and said in an unctuous voice, "You've been wise to diminish your cash position, Mr. Pērkons. Most of my clients are wishing they'd had your foresight in acquiring assets more suitable for the long run. We'll soon be lighting our cigars with *lats*."

Janis Pērkons took his time answering. "True, Mr. Lapsins. The Russians have imposed a ridiculous exchange rate, impoverishing most of us." Janis returned the loupe to its case and closed it with a methodical snap. Leaning back in his chair, he ran a hand over his goatee, looking thoughtful.

"Mr. Pērkons," Lapsins said. "In our many recent dealings, haven't my articles always proved genuine?"

"Genuinely overpriced," Janis said. He smiled as if he liked Lapsins, and smiled at another corner of the room as if someone else were there. "This is highway robbery!"

Kārlis, suddenly hot, tugged his collar loose. How could his father seem so at ease with these sharks?

Janis withdrew a gold cigarette case from his pocket. It popped open with spring-loaded action as he extended it toward the others, saying, "Personally, though, I'd rather be robbed by you than by the Communists."

"Come now. I like to think I'm providing a valuable service at great personal risk," Lapsins said, accepting a thin brown cigarette.

There was quiet laughter, the flick of a lighter and the ritual passing and puffing. Kārlis stopped watching when a floorboard above his head groaned. He stiffened, looking up. Someone was moving about in the upstairs living quarters. His antennae zeroed in on the stealthy footsteps while, inside the office, the men bantered about volume discounts, ruble versus lat, contraband-carrying surcharges and what the market would bear. They chatted casually, though Kārlis suspected every word was laced with cunning, and they seemed oblivious to the distressing footsteps Kārlis heard approaching.

"So, Mr. Pērkons, what have you decided?"

Kārlis didn't hear the answer. Panicked that an NKVD informant was coming, Kārlis fled down the steps to hide in the workshop. A parting glimpse into the office saw his father absorbed in counting out bills from a large roll of notes. Midway, Kārlis turned back¾should he burst into, what appeared to be, a high stakes currency crime to warn his father the spy was coming? No, the marketeers would react rashly. So, he crept back down, determined to forestall whoever was coming, to create a diversion if necessary, giving Papu time to hide the goods.

Near the foot of the stairs, Kārlis crouched behind some pallets while the apartment stairwell creaked under someone's weight. He strained to see who was there, chest clenched so tight he couldn't breathe. When he saw the unmistakable sasquatch-and-elfin figures of Eriks and Sniedze enter the workshop he could've strangled them.

"Eriks. Over here," Kārlis hissed, slicing the air with angry gestures until the two had joined him behind the pallets, Sniedze kneeling beside him. "What're you doing traipsing through the apartment! I told you about the spy. You're supposed to wait in the alley until I let you in."

Eriks who, much to Kārlis's annoyance, remained standing, said, "Yah, yah. We waited. What took so long? We figured something must've happened."

"Quiet. There are people up there with my father right now," Kārlis said, pointing to the loft.

The office door opened with a paralyzing click. A barrel-chested man in a pinstriped suit came out and, hands on hips, surveyed the workshop.

Next out was a clean-shaven fellow in a natty overcoat, the man called Lapsins. He descended the stairs with the spring of someone in expensive shoes. The office lamp went dark and Janis Pērkons exited, pausing to lock the door. He trotted downstairs after Lapsins and the corpulent bodyguard brought up the rear. Business must've concluded to their mutual satisfaction, Kārlis noted, somewhat awed by his father. The entrepreneurs were moving on now, shrewd and discreet as the velvet-feathered flight of owls at night.

Lapsins murmured to Janis as they passed where the boys hid, "They've bagged all the big game—factories, farms, the press. Then they took over the mid-sized companies and now, they're scraping the barrel, seizing the livelihood of even the small entrepreneur." His voice trailed as they went through the swinging doors that lead to the retail shop and the storefront.

"Time to close up shop, Mr. Pērkons. Lay low or get out of town—and by that I mean the country. The situation is far worse than we ever imagined."

Kārlis heard a muffled jingle, the bell on the shop door.

"Whew," Sniedze said after a moment's silence. "Where they going?"

"How should I know," Kārlis said. "*Ak tu kungs.* He might be back at any minute."

"Let's get the juice and get out of here," Eriks said.

Kārlis changed mental gears; he'd digest the transfer of treasure he'd just witnessed later. Carefully passing the cutting table in the dark, he took a key from its nail on the workbench. Eriks and Sniedze followed him back toward the immersion drums where he unlocked a cupboard and began scanning labels on the stocked shelves. "Chromium, ammonium sulphate, lime... Here." Denatured alcohol was stored on the lower shelf. He distributed two apiece.

"These are tiny," Eriks said, frowning at the liter-sized, brown bottles.

"What were you expecting? Barrels?"

"As long as I'm sticking my neck out, I might as well go down for a barrel as for a thimble-full."

"No one's going down—" Kārlis said, exasperated. How like Eriks to argue at the most inopportune— "That's the point. And this is considerably more than a thimbleful!"

"We're talking about torching the *kāpost galva* Corner House, not hosting a wiener roast," Eriks said. "We're gonna need more."

"How would we carry—"

"Like this," Eriks said, reaching past Kārlis and clanking several bottles together in each huge paw. He thrust them onto Sniedze, and turned for another grab.

"No. That's too obvious—" Kārlis said, crashing elbows with Eriks as he took them back from the witless Sniedze.

"Who goes there," came a voice.

Kārlis's head spun.

Light flickered across the workshop in a blinding flood. "Halt!" Igor Volkov, the Russian apprentice-spy, was staring at him, chest thrust out, at the cutting table.

Stung at first, to be yelled at on his own turf, Kārlis recovered, blinking. He stepped forward, hoping to screen Eriks and Sniedze, both hunched over clanking bottles behind his back.

"I said Halt," Volkov said. "Don't move." His hands were in plain view and, to Kārlis's relief, weaponless. His brown forelock looked disheveled and his shirt was untucked, like he'd been disturbed from a nap.

What a phony, Kārlis thought, a bitter taste rising in his throat. He was after all, only as old as Kārlis, but wielding the authority of the skull-crushing Soviet regime.

"Halt yourself," Kārlis wanted to say, but didn't. He plucked an awl off the workbench and faced Igor Volkov quietly from the opposite end of the cutting table. The two were similar in height, but the Russian had more muscle.

"So it's you," Volkov said. "What are you doing in cupboard."

"I live here, remember?" Kārlis said. "This is *Pērkons* Leather Works."

"I am superior here, not you," Volkov said. "You are trespasser and thief. Put your hands up."

"I'm the trespasser?" Kārlis said, amazed by the gall. "I'm supposed to be here. My duties require my attention at all hours. Somebody has to check those drums."

"You steal from state," Volkov said, pointing at Kārlis. "You back there," he called from behind the safety of the cutting table. "Step away from storage. What are you hiding?"

Kārlis didn't turn to see, but the clinking of glass added to his growing sense of calamity.

"I said Step Away." As Volkov advanced, a faint, familiar *thwop* came from his feet. Kārlis looked down.

"What in hell—," Kārlis began. Incredulous, he stepped back to see under the table. It took a moment to compute what he saw; it was so unexpected and disgusting. "You're wearing my slippers," Kārlis said, pointing the awl at the spy's feet. He stared at Volkov's eyes, daring him to deny it. "Who are you calling Thief."

A ripple of embarrassment crossed the Russian's face, seeming to knock him off balance for a moment.

"I know your scheme is to colonize the country," Kārlis said, hoping Eriks and Sniedze would pull themselves together while he blathered. "Get rid of us and move into our homes and livelihoods. But even into our shoes!"

"No need to colonize what already belongs to us," Volkov said, arrogance restored.

"That's such a lie," Kārlis said, vaguely concerned he was crossing a line. "You re-writing history?"

"No need to. Look around. Reality is outside of door. Statue of Mother Russia sits in middle of Lenin Boulevard. Is fact."

"The Freedom Monument?" Kārlis said, puffing with heat. "What a pervert you are."

"That's Mother of *Latvia*," Sniedze piped up, from behind Kārlis's elbow with a bulging, clinking rucksack slung over his shoulder.

"Mother *Russia*," Volkov said coolly. "Holding three stars, the Baltics, *in her hands*."

"A lie." Kārlis couldn't stop himself. "You try to look legitimate with rigged elections and changing the names of things in the middle of the night. You're a nation of liars led by a psychopath. And you don't know a *kāpost galva* thing about running a leather works."

Volkov smiled. He had a way of turning up the corners of his mouth while looking deadly.

"I have plenty experience," Igor Volkov said, idly picking up a strap of leather cut for a belt. He doubled it over and jerked the ends, making it snap. "You know Kalnins Bridge & Iron, I think?"

Kārlis's mouth went dry. Peters Kalnins's family business.

"Thought you might," Volkov said, eyes narrow. "Overfed fascists. Believe me, they were not what they appeared to be. I report them. The Cheka is pleased. Sends me here."

Kārlis started to feel shaky. Was this ratfink somehow responsible for Peters's arrest? And next he'd report Papu? He leaned against the cutting table to shore up his nerves.

Volkov stood there stretching and curling his fingers on the leather strap, looking titillated by Kārlis's sick reaction.

With a couple of deep breaths Kārlis was no longer shaking. Hatred was making him calm and murderous. He ignored the tugging on his sleeve.

"Let's go," Sniedze said, smelling of urine. "He must've did something to Peters. Come on."

"You in the big coat," Volkov shouted, looking toward Eriks. "Come out here with your hands up."

Eriks complied, emerging from the storage area, straightening to his full height.

Seeing Eriks's mass, Volkov took a step back, his pupils shrinking to pinpricks. "Stop right there," he ordered. "Show me your pockets."

Eriks looked strangely complacent as he opened the edges of his overcoat. "It's camel," he said, pivoting from side to side like a coat model. "The color is called camel. It's an alpaca blend, herringbone weave, double breasted wool number from Stockholm."

"His family owns the finest store in Riga," Sniedze blurted stupidly.

"Is that so?" Volkov said. "Well, it's mine now. Put it on the table."

Kārlis expected a mouthy retort. Instead, he saw Eriks's eyes go dark, a flex in his oversized frame.

Volkov noticed it too. "All I have to do is whistle," he said tightly." The Cheka will hunt you down. At your finest store in Riga."

Eriks walked to Volkov's end of the table. About to remove his coat, he seemed to change his mind. "But what if you can't whistle?" he said. "What if your jaw is pulverized to slop so you can't tattle on Peters or anybody else ever again?"

"You can't be so stupid you'd threaten me," Volkov said, eyes flitting sideways.

With a couple of giant strides, Eriks was behind the Russian, blocking his escape with arms spread like gaping jaws.

Kārlis tightened his grip on the awl and also closed in, determined Volkov not pass him without first getting stabbed in the throat. He felt like he wasn't in his head, but was witnessing the scene from the rafters, watching himself and Eriks cut out a cancerous tumor.

Volkov's eyes looked like white plates, seeing too late he was surrounded.

Do it. Be rid of him. A chemical in Kārlis's blood urged killing him now, fast and final. The opportunity wouldn't come again.

A muffled jingle came from the storefront, dully tugging Kārlis back within the boundaries of his usual self. Killer Kārlis kept screaming to slay or be slain.

Eriks also seemed in suspended animation, a bombshell in midair.

Kārlis's father pushed through the swinging doors, taking in the lit up workshop and the cornered apprentice-spy.

"*Sveikee.* Everybody," Janis Pērkons boomed, breaking up the testosterone vortex with a cheery greeting.

Seeing his father instantly reminded Kārlis of who he was.

No one moved for a second. Chests heaved.

Kārlis lowered his awl. He was not a murderer.

Janis acted like nothing was amiss. "It's good of you boys to help out in the shop this evening," he said, taking center stage, thumbs in his vest pockets. "I like that initiative." He nodded at each of them. "It's an extremely busy time. Seems everybody wants to buy a suitcase." To Volkov he said, "I see you've met my son."

Janis grabbed Kārlis in a rowdy bear hug. Rubbing his knuckles over his head, a gesture Kārlis hated, Janis whispered, "What's wrong with you! Don't antagonize him." Kārlis was released, a moment later, to find Eriks and Volkov still locked in icy stares.

Janis said, "Boys, Igor has recently moved here from—er, Russia. You're practically the same age! Probably have much in common." Janis stood between them all, sizing up the situation as if deciding which bill of goods to sell.

"He said the Freedom Monument represents Mother Russia," chirped Sniedze, pointing at Igor.

Janis raised his eyebrows. "You boys are worked up about a *statue*? That's funny," he said, shaking his head. "When I was seventeen we got a bang out of horseracing."

"It's mother of Latvia," Sniedze said, piously.

"Oh, who's to say," Janis said, a gruff edge to his voice. "Let's drop it."

Igor Volkov lifted his eyes, as if he alone could see something funny in the roof beams. "Your son is stealing inventory," he said.

Kārlis met his father's gaze, sobered by the concern he saw there, when his head exploded, hit so hard his skull lifted off his neck. He dropped the awl, gasped, saw sparks of light, fumbled, clutching the cutting table.

"He has smart mouth," Volkov said, cradling the knuckles of his right hand. Then his fist hooked deep and hard into Kārlis's belly.

Suddenly Kārlis's face was on the cutting table, viewing the wood grain from the other end of a slick, throbbing nose. Shocked, hunched over, he couldn't pull air into his lungs.

Volkov was talking.

Noisy protests, his father, friends.

Words didn't register. He was going to puke as soon as breath returned.

The belt lashed his face like a fist of fire.

Kārlis tried to defend his face but arms held guts. He couldn't see. Eyes blurred, hot, stinging.

"Next time I tell you to do something, Citizen, hop to it."

Kārlis tried. Waved his hands feebly in front of himself.

The backs of his knees buckled. His body dropped to the floor, humiliation passing fast under a kick to the kidney and the lash, this time ripping his ear, burning. Slash at shoulder dulled by coat. Kick to head jarred brain, teeth clattered. Curl up.

Volkov whipped Kārlis's head in a furious onslaught.

Kārlis curled tighter. Was that him screaming? Blows pelted his back. Acute, throbbing deep inside, horribly wrong.

"No, Eriks!" His father's voice. "Don't touch him or we're all dead!"

Something about slippers.

"I said Are These Your Slippers?" Volkov cried. Another kick. "What?"

Torrent in head blurred sounds.

Sniedze was shrill, "Stop him, he'll kill him."

His father, shouting, "—some misunderstanding, I apologize—"

"What?" yelled Volkov.

Kārlis braced, but the whip split his face. He sobbed.

"No," Kārlis said.

"What?"

"No," Kārlis said. "Yours. Your slippers." He was crying.

Pray the beating would stop.

Answered by a kick in the guts.

Lolling head, light through blood-bleary slits. "Your slippers," Kārlis moaned.

"That's what I thought," Volkov said, standing over his head.

Ceiling swirl. Father watching, holding back Eriks.

Volkov folded the strap. "Get them out of here," he told Janis, snapping the leather.

"You gonna be all right, Mr. Pērkons?" Sniedze's high-pitched voice. "You're awful white."

"I'm—" his father said, "Just get Kārlis to a doctor."

Kārlis heard feet moving through the cement under his ear. He didn't want to move. Hands grabbed his armpits. He screamed going up, limp and soaked. Heart drumming in ears, muffled the jangle of keys, the door scraping open to the alley.

He was ushered into the freezing night air on the unevenly matched shoulders of Eriks and Sniedze. He felt he was flying, then slamming back into his body with the throb of each cell and nerve.

"I could've stopped him, Mr. Pērkons," Eriks said. "You should've let me."

"That—that boy is a representative of the Soviet regime." His father's low voice was trembling. "If anything happens to him, the Cheka will kill us."

Kārlis felt his father's hand on his shoulder.

"Now that that's out of his system," Janis said, "it's possible he won't harm us further. He doesn't matter."

Kārlis couldn't lift his head or return his father's goodbye. It hurt to raise his feet over the icy sludge of the alley. Every step was an ordeal, a marathon. Eriks supported his slow progress while Sniedze strove not to get in the way. Finally they turned out of the alley, where the sidewalks of Lenin Boulevard were smoother. Eriks decided it would be faster to carry Kārlis on his back, his hands under Kārlis's knees. Kārlis grasped his friend's neck and braced himself for the jarring pain of Eriks's stride.

"Someone's there. Up ahead," Sniedze said, stopping cold.

"It's just the painters again, see?" Eriks said. "There's the guy dragging the ladder."

"Yah," Sniedze said. "There's a sign—" Sniedze stopped with a sharp intake of breath. "They're not painters. Look. Oh God. Oh, God," Sniedze whimpered.

"Quiet," Eriks said.

"I'm not going past that," Sniedze said with a tinge of hysteria.

Eriks shrank against the side of the building. "No. We'll backtrack," he whispered, "and go another way."

The night was so quiet, even the wind had died to a light breeze. Kārlis couldn't imagine why Eriks was spooked. He opened his eyes the best he could and strained to see. From the glow of a streetlamp, a white rectangle shone from across the street, under some trees in the park. It looked like a sign, swaying. Trying to read it, the dark setting came into focus. The sign was posted on a man hanging by the neck.

"What's it say," Sniedze said.

Eriks whispered, "Capitalist."

Alone in the workshop, Igor Volkov stood shaking, titillated, breathing hard, and feeling magnificent.

Pērkons returned from the alley. Shoulders slumped under the fancy suit, he rolled the workshop door shut and locked it. Turning rigidly, he cast a searing glare at Igor.

Igor met the hateful stare. How dare Pērkons judge him? The capitalist Pērkons, if anybody, should understand opportunities had to be made from whatever at hand, no half measures. In Pērkons's echelon, you must be the one kicking, not the fool cringing on the ground. Igor was herculean, increased in power daily. But Latvians were a weak, spoiled species. He vowed to punish them.

Finally Pērkons broke eye contact and went to a cupboard.

"Weakness is a plague," Igor told Pērkons's back. "Weak people don't deserve rights. They must be checked in order to prevent future generations from falling into degeneracy."

To Igor's astonishment, the wealthy man dropped to his knees and wiped blood off the floor.

Igor turned to climb the stairs, unhurried, to the sleeping quarters, unafraid of reprisals. Scuffing in Kārlis Pērkons's deerskin and boiled wool slippers, Igor's toes throbbed after jamming Kārlis's ribs and soft belly, pleasantly, a sensation lost when wearing boots. But next time there would be boots. New, heavy duty, Latvian-stomping boots.

Igor quartered in the son's room, at the end of the hall hung with weavings. Next assignment he would require the master's bedroom. Pērkons had a king's bed, furs on the floor, and a door to a private running-water bathtub. But Igor was drawn to the son's room with sick fascination. Same age as the spoiled "artist", he and Kārlis Pērkons occupied separate realities. Snooping through the rotten little prick's belongings had given Igor an outrageous new view of the bourgeoisie that proved the true extent of the cruel injustice he'd suffered.

Igor closed the bedroom door and stood before the dresser mirror. Symmetrical facial features, cheeks blazing, lips full, he averted eyes from the handsome reflection of a superior being inexplicably and unjustly outcast from human community. "When I get the army uniform, all will see my true magnificence," he told himself. His talent was wasted in the Komsomol, the Communist youth helpers. Anger for not yet being selected by the military, darkened his mood.

His gaze riveted to a photograph stuck under the mirror frame. The stiff paper emitted a whiff of chemical fixative as Igor examined it. God Almighty. Did Pērkons have another house? That must be where the wife and girl were sent. Stalwart stone building blocks, it was an enormous, country manor on an expanse of grass and flowers. Over the balcony leaned a gang of feisty-looking young men, Igor's age, lined up from tallest to shortest. He'd never seen an image so shiny, sharp, stylish, modern.

Igor was gripped and incensed that Pērkons owned such a camera. The value must be astronomical. Since Pērkons, the blatant profligate, was not a photographer by trade, the camera must be a toy or hobby, used to flaunt his lavish excess and goad rivals to jealousy. Igor had been examining the photograph earlier that night, seething resentment, when he'd heard creaking from downstairs and policed the premises. He'd not only caught Kārlis Pērkons stealing, he'd recognized his cohort thieves from this picture. He'd thought of the picture while kicking Kārlis Pērkons senseless. Perhaps the photograph was why he'd kept kicking.

He recognized one face mugging for the camera. Knowing the guy made Riga feel like a small village Igor had already mastered. The tall one was Peters Kalnins. Igor knew this because the Komsomol had assigned him to Kalnins Bridge & Iron, and he'd reported captain-of-the-hockey-team Peters to the NKVD as a Harmful Element. Next to him was the dangerous oaf he'd just seen downstairs. Only instead of the coveted coat he wore a leafy Latvian holiday hat. Igor was determined to know that one's name. He could demand Pērkons tell him the name, or track the boy through the family-owned luxury store touted in the foolish boast. Next in the line of enemies were two with dark hair, arms around each other in horseplay. One muscled, one effeminate. Hmm. They were unknown to Igor. He scorned the next, the white-haired boy who stared down the lens with a cerebral conceit. Then stood Kārlis Pērkons, whose head Igor had just used as a football. Igor smirked at the wry insolent expression seen through the camera. Pērkons's bloody face was not so cocky now. Last was the runt of the pack. He'd also been downstairs tonight, screaming like a little girl.

The photograph had a profound effect on Igor, underscoring his understanding of how the world worked in hierarchies. Some people were better than others, more admirable than everyone else, having a better time and, like these young men, probably enjoying pleasurable sex lives with beautiful blond Latvian girls. Igor permitted a desperate fantasy. He imagined himself on that balcony, standing at the prestigious end, the tallest one of all.

His mouth soured at reality. He could steal Kārlis Pērkons's shoes, hang a smart army uniform in another man's closet, but he would never be admitted to that balcony, never wear the casual expression that bespoke the confidence of belonging, the look he could see even on the runt's freckled face. Igor wanted to rip that photograph into a million shreds, but stayed his hand. He would do better. He would destroy those pictured. He could do it. He would crush those boys like the gravel on his path to eminence. He imagined the balcony after what it deserved, a blood bath. His hand trembled as he shoved the picture back under the mirror frame. He wanted to do horrible things, wanted to inflict pain on all gentry... wanted to kill them all slowly, wanted to strip the skins off their flesh.

Hand of Death, K. Smiltens. 1945

- 5 -

DECEMBER 22, 1940

IT WAS STILL DARK THE next morning when Janis
Pērkons rolled the workshop doors open. Cold air
stung the freshly shaved skin around his goatee as he
looked into the alley. His two employees were already
out there shoveling. Edgars, his devoted master craftsman, and Guntis, the dapper retail clerk, spread snow
over the bald and slushy spots to prepare a uniform
surface for the arrival of the sledge.

Edgars exhaled sharply. "Oh it's you, Mr. Pērkons,"
he said. "I thought you were, you know, the *apprentice.*"

"He's still asleep," Janis said. "Big night." Last night
he'd allowed a Soviet hoodlum to lash his son's face
and kick him senseless. The memory was agonizing.

Janis grabbed a shovel, as if manual labor might
work the remorse from his spirit. He reviewed the
event incessantly and still didn't see what he could've
done differently. Bodily injuries could heal. But if that
Russian punk had a scratch or a bruise or even a bad
taste in his mouth when he reported to his NKVD

superiors... Were the rumors of summary execution overblown? Janis didn't want to find out.

"This is good," Edgars said, gathering the shovels and heading inside. "Don't worry, Mr. Pērkons. We'll load those pallets so fast it'll be like they were never here."

Janis nodded approval, looking up and down the alley. There was no sign of the buyer. He checked his pocket watch. Chest bound with worry, Janis lit a cigarette and paced, turning his mind from his son to easier calculations. What cash might be squeezed from the remaining inventory? Could he get away with selling the tools and the drums? Could he find a trustworthy buyer? The state would be watching closely, as leather production was essential to transportation, to soldiering, to war. On the other hand, divesting the capital equipment would stop the revenue stream. He didn't want to do that prematurely, just because of nerves. Hold the course. Maybe he had more time.

An indistinct groan and the beat of horse hooves made him look down the alley where a dark shape grew larger, the buyer's sledge. Janis threw down his cigarette and adjusted wire-rimmed spectacles.

"Let's make a deal," Janis said.

Edgars rolled the workshop doors open slowly, avoiding the screech.

The sledge was suddenly there; two horses pulling a triangular rig on wide iron runners. Janis recognized the driver, a longstanding customer, and directed him to the loading bay. Edgars and Guntis hustled out pallets of leather goods and secured the cargo. In the sensory rush that peaks during the commission of a capital offense, Janis stepped on the runner and said to the driver. "Your next order will be ready in a fortnight."

One of the horses whinnied loudly and stamped.

"No," the driver said, looking up and down the alley,

forehead glistening with sweat. "No, we can't do this again."

Janis hid his disappointment.

"Boots. Holsters. Harnesses. Saddle bags. It's all there," Edgars said, thumping the stacked pallets. "We've thrown in assorted straps and hides."

The driver held out a thick envelope.

Adrenaline pumped as Janis took it, briefly thumbing the contents. He nodded at the driver and they parted with claps on the back.

Edgars helped turn the horses into the alley. Forceful white streams of condensation billowed from the animals' nostrils as they pulled away. Then he rolled the doors together.

Janis watched the sledge grow smaller as possibly his last customer faded into the half-light of a morning that held dim prospects for brightening. He checked the other direction. No one was there. Stepping inside the workshop, Janis rubbed his hands vigorously. Edgars closed the door behind him, snapping the lock. It appeared they hadn't been caught. Breathing deeply, the fragrances of leather and Neatsfoot oil soothed Janis's tight chest. Composed, he peeled a slab of bills from the payment envelope and gave it to Edgars.

The old man's hands trembled as he pocketed the money.

Guntis then reached for his cut, but froze midway, his eyes glued to something over Janis's shoulder.

Janis turned. The informant, Igor Volkov, was leaning against the wall watching, eyelids at half-mast. Janis hadn't heard him come down the stairs. He could've seen the whole deal.

Pushing the pad of cash into Guntis's hand, Janis demonstrated that they were to act like they had nothing to hide.

Volkov ambled over, eyes widening with interest.

Pivoting abruptly, Guntis fled through the swinging doors to the retail shop. Edgars was suddenly absorbed with a half-finished suitcase splayed over the cutting table.

"What's going on here?" Volkov said.

Janis cleared his throat. "People can't get enough of Edgars's luggage," he said, thinking fast how to placate the informant, to stop his going to his superiors. "In the old days we'd say Business is Booming."

Janis cut another stack of bills from the envelope with the same measured movements he'd done for Edgars and Guntis, and handed it to Volkov. "From each according to his ability, to each according to his need," Janis said, bandying a Communist motto.

Volkov was inscrutable. Janis found it impossible to comprehend the Russian mind, but if it was the glint of greed enlivening those black eyes, then Janis could speak his language.

Finally, to Janis's relief, Volkov grabbed the cash. When he did, Janis saw his hand was red and swollen from beating Kārlis.

Volkov folded the bills and slid the wad into his trouser pocket.

Edgars struck a rivet and it rang like a bell.

Disguising his loathing, Janis extracted tobacco from his vest and offered Volkov a smoke.

Volkov took a cigarette, eyes lingering on the gold cigarette case.

Janis scraped a wooden match across the cutting table and held the flame out to Volkov before he lit his own.

"Igor," Janis said, "like you, I started as an apprentice."

Volkov was still staring at the gold case.

Article 58

"The satisfaction of creating something with your hands is at the core of this business," Janis said, spinning the cigarette case on the cutting table. The whirling gold seemed to mesmerize the young Communist, who watched it silently. "I suggest you get comfortable in the workshop today," Janis said. "Make a belt and a few simple items for yourself." Janis felt ill at the memory of the belt lashing Kārlis's face, but he kept on buttering. "With a bit of practice you can even make yourself some slippers." Janis bit his tongue. He recalled slippers had somehow been a point of contention in last night's brawl. He knew that the past decade in Russia had seen an acute shortage of leather, which led to a government ban on the private production of shoes. Russians could only purchase poor quality state-made shoes, which fell apart quickly. Had his son hit some footwear raw nerve that had nearly cost him his life?

"Anyway," Janis said, exhaling a stream of smoke, "Learn from the master. Edgars here can make anything out of leather."

"Is that so!" Volkov was at the workbench in a blink, nearly knocking Edgars off balance. "Can you make stew from a belt?" He fingered the laid out leather and bore into the old craftsman with his black eyes. "It's culinary specialty where I come from."

Edgars shrank back, bewildered, his craggy face creased in shock.

Volkov poked Edgars in the chest with a forefinger. "Since you can make anything, I demand you prepare belt stew, old man. And it better be tender because you are going to eat it."

"No need to be repulsive," Janis shouted, outraged by the abuse. He and Edgars exchanged looks. They were dealing with a fiend.

"As for you, cobbler," Volkov spat, rounding on Janis, "I require a pair of boots, strong, shiny, superior boots. As tribute to dear Comrade Stalin, the workmanship must be the best anyone has ever seen."

Janis nodded his head. Not so much agreeing to the boots, but in understanding that he was not submitting merely to state police, as if the NKVD weren't bad enough. This individual was sick in the head. He pulled a deep drag of smoke. There was no percentage in being furious with a lunatic, and no way to predict his moves.

"And don't bother tutoring me about your skins, Citizen," Volkov rebuked. "This foul, ragged shoe shop is just a temporary assignment until I can join the army. That's a career for men. Not making things people wear under their feet."

"You're right, of course," Janis said, impressed by the civility of his own voice. "Comrade." With a parting nod he turned to go to his office.

He left the gold case on the cutting-table altar, hopefully sufficient sacrifice to cover the morning's free-enterprising sins.

Climbing the stairs to the loft felt like scaling a mountain. Janis closed the door behind him and leaned against it, wrestling his collar loose. He calmed himself by looking at the photograph of his family. *Anna, Kārlis and Biruta.* The reasons for everything he did. Breath flowed again.

Suddenly Janis was struck by the memory of last night's meeting with the gem dealer. He hadn't thought about it once since walking into a shit storm between the kids and that junior representative of the NKVD. Unlocking the desk drawer, he was relieved to see the velvet bag of treasure where he'd left it.

Plopping in the desk chair, he unlaced his right boot. Edgars had crafted these boots according to

Janis's specifications with secret compartments in the heel, accessed from the inside. He filled the heel compartment with jewels, pushed it closed, and replaced the inner sole. The knee-high fleece lining concealed long, slender pouches. He filled them with half the gold chains, adjusted the fleece lining and re-laced the boot tightly. Nothing was visible. He stashed the remainder of the gold and the cash from the morning sale in the other boot.

Minutes later he emerged from his office wearing his fur hat and overcoat, and locked the door.

The workshop was empty when he came down. The cutting table bare, the offering accepted. Maybe that bought more time.

Janis passed through the swinging doors to find Edgars standing in the showroom looking funereal.

"He left a minute ago," Edgars said. "The apprentice. Wish I knew where he was going."

Janis shook his head, not knowing if having the spy hanging around the premises was more or less worrisome than not knowing his whereabouts.

Guntis was refreshing the merchandise in the window with the same pride he'd always taken in the task. The display of boots, suitcases and equestrian tack looked, to Janis, like a friend on his deathbed. Pērkons Leather Works, decades of sweat and sacrifice, for what? Janis moved leadenly, a heaviness that had nothing to do with the gold in his boots.

"Good day, Mr. Pērkons," Edgars said as he left, ever his supporter.

Bells jingled as Janis closed the wood-framed glass door behind him.

He'd barely gone ten steps before thin trembling fingers grabbed his arm. "Mr. Pērkons!" said a scarecrow of a man, bony and ragged, with straw-colored hair.

Catching his breath, Janis saw the scarecrow push something in his face. His eyes focused on a gold band, probably a wedding ring.

Scarecrow whispered hoarsely, "Someone said you'd give me a fair price for this."

Someone said. Janis recoiled at the words, pushing the stranger's arm away.

Someone said rang in his head like a fire alarm.

"Must be a mistake," Janis said, looking around to see who was watching.

"Please sir," the scarecrow persisted.

"You'd do better keeping the gold," Janis whispered, chest pumping.

"I've got to buy potatoes." Desperate eyes flashed at Janis. "They want cash. We've got to eat. Take it. Take it," the man said, pushing the ring on Janis. It fell in his pocket.

The seconds required to pull off a number of bills while keeping his roll out of sight, seemed like interminable exposure in the public square. Janis looked around furtively as he paid the man.

Stalking away, Janis's chest was bound up with anger at himself for being caught off guard. Some fool had endangered his painstakingly wrought plans, exploiting a tendency he had to help others. Everyone was out for himself, Janis saw, bristling, every man a threat. Janis steeled up, trying to forget the desperation in the man's eyes.

Sympathy was unaffordable.

He couldn't help everyone. Janis saw with sadness that his foresight rent a chasm between himself and the ill prepared, separating him from most of his countrymen.

Article 58

Kāpost galva Russians. *Kāpost galva* wedding rings, filthy lifeblood of the black market. The band weighed in his pocket like the headstone of a mass grave.

The sidewalk was filling as the bleak light of morning took hold of the neighborhood. A line of people stood outside the grocery store though it wasn't open yet. In the cafe, men sipped little cups of strong coffee while standing at tall counters. The tailor waved at Janis through the lighted window of his shop, his mouth full of pins, reworking a jacket on a dress form. The bookseller wore a glazed, vacant expression as he leaned against the doorframe of his near-empty store that had recently been purged of all inappropriate titles.

Janis did a double take at the corner. The street name had changed overnight, from Freedom to Lenin. How fitting. He barely recognized his neighborhood. More and more storefronts were vacant, abandoned. Janis imagined each darkened door meant an arrest, a deportation or, if rumors were true, an execution. It was only a matter of time before Pērkons Leather Works would get a visit from the Cheka. He continued down the block, stony as the gargoyles perched above him.

"Announcement! Announcement!" came an amplified voice from a tinny sounding public address system.

Janis stopped mid-step. He didn't move, except to turn in the direction of the voice.

A military-type stepped on a small, impromptu platform on the sidewalk so everyone else was eye level to his tall black boots as they gathered around him. It was becoming a regular choreography on Freed– Lenin Boulevard.

Janis and other passersby waited obediently, listening.

"Citizens are required to attend all scheduled labor rallies," the speaker said, scanning the crowd. "There we proclaim the equality and brotherhood of nations." He slapped a black riding crop into the open palm of his glove. "We will show the world how, since the Latvian nation expressed the ardent wish to join the USSR's fraternal family of nations and the Supreme Soviet unanimously agreed to accept that request, the Soviet and Latvian flags now fly side by side."

The crowd was silent. A couple of people clapped.

"Side by side," Janis thought. "Everybody's happy."

"Citizens are required to attend all rallies in support of the fight for a better future, a fight for the ideals of Marx, Engels, Lenin and Stalin." He slapped the whip, watching the reaction of the audience like a hawk sizing up rodents.

Clearly the purpose of the speech was to identify dissenters, the next candidates for purging. So Janis hid his disgust, trying to look mindless and blend in with the anonymous mass.

"I appeal to the working people of Riga to be helpful in the detection of hostile elements," the speaker concluded with a final smack of the riding crop against his boots.

The crowd was dismissed and shuffled off.

"You there! You!" The speaker descended the platform with alacrity. "I want to see your identity papers!" He stalked past Janis to detain a portly, older man wearing a fur lapel and a black band on his fedora. The gentleman looked flustered, obediently accessing pockets to produce his papers.

Janis moved away in terror-relief, struck by the capricious, bullying regime that stopped one man for a spot search and let another go. He slouched and slowed his usual brisk pace to blend in with the crowd. Head down, he boarded a streetcar and found a seat by the window.

Article 58

Janis wanted to patronize an underground coin dealer twenty blocks away, irked that last night the gem trafficker had got the better of him. Passing the Freedom Monument en route, he twisted in his seat to admire Mother of Latvia, who'd been threatened with the wrecking ball. She towered above the surrounding treetops in her green gown of oxidized copper, the troublemaker. Guards patrolled her travertine pedestal, forbidding newlyweds to lay flowers there. She persisted in reminding everybody that Latvia was a sovereign nation. But her stoic eyes accused Janis of betraying his son for the sake of keeping the doors to business open.

Turrets and spires overshadowed the twisty cobblestone streets leading to the coin dealer, who operated from an antique shop in the medieval heart of Old Riga. The stone faces and statuary carved into the tall, narrow buildings didn't impart their usual wisdom-of-the-centuries to Janis as he lingered, beleaguered, at a nearby cafe. For nearly two hours he'd observed the antique shop and its visitors. Finally he got up the nerve to go in with his illegal proposition. The dealer swiftly sold him ten United States Golden Eagles, each with a face value of twenty dollars. He pocketed the gold with his loose change and exited the antique shop, his chest hard as stone.

It was around two in the afternoon and the sun would soon be setting.

He rode the streetcar back to his usual stop and walked the remaining blocks toward the Leather Works. Every street sign he passed now bore the name

Lenin. Was it just yesterday the street was Freedom? He was exhausted.

"Mr. Pērkons!" Snip Cepurnieks, the tailor, was calling from the door of his shop. "Come back and have a cup of coffee with me."

"That would be excellent," Janis said.

He followed Cepurnieks into his shop and behind the counter. They passed bolts of fabric, a sewing machine, and a large mirror as they walked to the rear of the shop. Overstuffed armchairs surrounded a coffee percolator bubbling on a dainty woodstove. Wool gabardine, pinned in the shape of a suit jacket, hung on a tailor's mannequin. One section of wall was covered with layers of newspaper, making a pinboard in which pins, needles, and scissors were stuck.

The tailor chatted about the frigid weather while Janis hung up his overcoat.

Janis accepted a hot cup of coffee and a light for his cigarette and sat back in the armchair.

"Many of my customers seem to be missing," Cepurnieks said, extracting a pin from the pinboard and inserting it deftly into the jacket, repeating the motion over and over. "The city officials have been dismissed and replaced by, well, jailbirds. People with little regard for the decorum of public office, no sense of style." He sighed. "Latvia may never again see the exquisite couture of my former clientele, and that's a damn shame."

Janis was uneasy with the conversation. It was illegal to criticize Communist officials, even their fashion sense. "I haven't given it much thought," he said.

Cepurnieks swooshed his creation off the mannequin with a flourish, and strode to the sewing machine where he positioned the jacket under the needle.

Article 58

Janis sipped coffee and watched cigarette smoke swirl around the headless dummy. The yellowed news articles from the pinboard caught his eye. There was a photo of Adolf Hitler, triumphant after his *blitzkrieg* invasion of Poland, old news; and one of Josef Stalin in full military regalia. The two dictators reminded Janis of giant chess players manipulating smaller countries over Europe's checkerboard, millions of destroyed lives incidental to the game.

Cepurnieks raised his voice over the drone of the sewing machine. "The only people who can afford a good suit now want to wear military uniforms. But I tell you, a well-tailored uniform in itself advances a man through the ranks. Look how the raspberry piping on the collar and cuffs here adds zip to this olive green wool."

The coffee was bracing. Seeing that Cepurnieks was thoroughly engrossed at the sewing machine, Janis loosened the laces of his boots and added the newly acquired gold.

Cepurnieks chattered on, "I'll pull through this. The Communists don't want my shop. Factories, farms, publishers, yah, of course. But I'm an owner-operator, a one-man show. They'll leave me alone. Hold the course, that's my recommendation. This mess will blow over."

Raising an eyebrow at Janis, Cepurnieks said, "Tell me, Mr. Pērkons, how did you know to sell your holdings while prices were high?"

It had been obvious to Janis. Last year sixty thousand ethnic Germans had sold their properties and left the country. Something was up. He'd followed suit. Then, Boom. The Soviets had come in like it had all been pre-arranged. Janis shrugged. "Lucky, I guess."

"It's businessmen like you, Mr. Pērkons, who have outside employees and the means of production that the Communists want," the tailor said, "Or don't want, however you look at it. They say you are exploiting the working class. That you're an Enemy of the People." Cepurnieks spoke around a mouthful of pins. Clanging bells alerted the tailor to someone at the front door. Excusing himself, he went to the counter.

Janis blew smoke, perturbed to be considered an Enemy of the People when all he did was take risks on behalf of others and work his tail off. Of course, he knew it applied to anyone who doubted the rightness of the Party Line. He sipped his coffee, until loud unruly voices arrested the cup halfway to his lips.

The men who'd entered the shop had breached the front counter and were approaching where he sat. Janis jettisoned his cigarette in his coffee cup and hid at the side of the room behind a large mirror. Peering through bolts of fabric he saw three NKVD agents pushing a whimpering, disheveled woman out of view of the public, toward where Janis had been sitting.

Cepurnieks acknowledged the tear-streaked, shaking woman was a customer, admitting he'd finished a remnant dress for her the previous day.

Janis's eyes were drawn to the guns. Each Chekist wore one within a quick grab. That's what made him feel like a bug about to be squished.

"Citizen Cepurnieks," said the NKVD, "this person informs us that you have willfully mutilated the image of General Secretary Stalin."

"What? No, Comrade! Never! I swear!" Cepurnieks said, aghast. "Madam, what is this?"

"Rebellion against the People," cut in the NKVD, "in person or in effigy, is against the law. Hostile elements are not tolerated." He twisted the woman's arm.

"It's there," she screamed, pointing to the newspapered pinboard.

Another agent strode over to inspect the board. There, amidst hundreds of pins, one had pierced the picture of General Secretary Josef Stalin, between the eyes. An ugly smile crossed the agent's face. "Citizen Cepurnieks, you did this?"

"I, well, I'm a tailor," Cepurnieks stammered. "It was nothing intentional. I don't even notice those articles. That's just where I keep my pins." He turned to the woman. "What did you tell them?"

"I saw you do it. I reported you." She was shrill. "I know how this works! You were testing me—testing my loyalty. You mutilate Stalin's picture in front of me and then you turn *me* in if I don't report it."

"Good God," Cepurnieks said, looking horrified. "Please, this is a mistake. I meant no harm. I beg you to give me another chance." His chest was heaving. "I can help you."

Janis's heart was pounding so hard he thought everyone in the shop would hear it.

"I'm loyal but I know people who aren't," the tailor said, wide-eyed and shiny with sweat. "I can give you names."

A scapegoat. The tailor would use him as a scapegoat, Janis saw, edging along the wall toward the back of the shop. He was afraid opening and closing the door to the alley would give away his presence, but the scraping noise seemed muffled by a shot, a scream and hysterical sobs.

Outside Janis stumbled into a snowdrift. He thought he'd vomit, but cold air quelled the urge. His steps toward the back entrance of Pērkons Leather Works were ragged, uneven. Holding his guts as he ran, he glimpsed over his shoulder. There was a figure in the alley, but nothing to do with him. Ducking into his workshop, he clutched the doorframe, gasping, teeth chattering. Only then did he ask himself why the door to the alley was open.

They had come. His heart dropped to his stomach like a chunk of ice. Time was up. His loft level office door was flung wide. Inside, a uniformed man was dumping the contents of drawers. Igor Volkov stood with him, erect and rapturous.

Guntis was below, wringing his hands. Janis might have run, but he followed the clerk's gaze to the cutting table where two men flanked Edgars. One held the old man's arms behind his back; a second held the photograph of Janis's family in front of Edgars' face, tapping the frame with a pistol.

Janis's knees went weak. Finally he found the strength to step forward.

"Comrade Officer," he said, "I'm the one you want. That man is a citizen and a worker."

Three sets of NKVD eyes burned into Janis as the Communists pushed Edgars away and rounded on him.

"You are Janis Pērkons, claiming to be the owner of Pērkons Leather Works?"

Janis's ears still were ringing from the gunshot fired at the tailor, the preview to his fate.

"Yah, Comrade. I am," he said. It was over now.

He tuned out the ranting of the NKVD agent. The thug held his family photograph. Focus on their faces, he thought. *Anna, Kārlis, and Biruta.* Janis's chest rose and fell more easily as he thought of them. He regretted not standing up for his son last night. He would rather that have been Kārlis's last memory of him.

The sentimental distraction ended when the agent threw the photograph down, speaking rapidly while glass shattered. "By the authority vested in me by the USSR and by General Secretary Stalin I hereby nationalize this establishment in the name of the People of the USSR. I order you to place the entire contents of your pockets on the counter."

The Communists puffed up, as if hoping Janis might resist.

"Empty your pockets," echoed one of them.

Janis didn't argue. He fished his keys and some loose change from his trousers, setting them on the counter with the deliberation a man would summon for his last mortal act. He pulled his watch from his vest pocket, the chain rustled as he tugged it loose and laid it down. There was a package of tobacco and a clip of folded bills in his inside coat pocket and—oh, the gold ring.

One guy knocked Janis off balance and pushed him against the cutting table to pat him down—humiliating.

"Now leave. Immediately," the officer said. "Any attempt by you to return here will rightfully be viewed as trespassing and burglary and will be prosecuted by the Riga NKVD as a criminal offense."

Janis was frozen to the spot. Had he heard correctly?

"Do you understand?"

He must have looked as dazed as he felt. The officer was yelling now.

"Leave the premises, Citizen Pērkons. Do not return unless you want to be arrested."

Without endangering his employees with a look of farewell, Janis Pērkons walked away.

K. Smiltens, 1947.

- 6 -

KĀRLIS WOKE, FOR A MOMENT not remembering
where he was. The crack under the door lit up stacked
flour bags and a shelf of baking ingredients across from
where he lay. Rolling over, ribs screamed! *Ak tu kungs!*
Never move again. He pressed two fingers against his
neck. Hard to tell if his pulse was weaker now than
the last time he checked. Pulling the blanket under his
chin, he nestled his head onto the salt bag pillow, listening to the murmur of voices outside the pantry and
wallowing in his miserable failures.

The door opened making Kārlis wince at the light.
It was Mr. Leopolds again. Squatting in front of the
wide shelf where Kārlis bunked, the baker prodded and
pressed at Kārlis's ribs and abdomen.

"That hurts," Kārlis moaned.

"He gave it to you in the kishka," Mr. Leopolds said.
"The no-goodnik. He should lie in the earth."

"My pulse is weak, Mr. Leopolds," Kārlis said. "You
can be straight with me."

Mr. Leopolds flipped a switch. "You're not as bad
as all that," he said, parting Kārlis's eyelids with a

thumb and forefinger. He shaded Kārlis's pupils with his hand. Then he bared them to the glare of the light bulb, nodding at the reaction. "Eyes look like rotten plums, but functional. The schnozz is not broken, so you'll still have your pretty face." He pressed a cold cloth against the lash welts on Kārlis's neck, saying, "And the girls are gonna love these tough-guy stripes."

The girls! Kārlis shrank with fresh horror and humiliation. Lileja Lipkis was bound to hear about his pathetic performance. He wanted to stay in this closet for the rest of his wretched life.

Mr. Leopolds turned off the light and went out to the kitchen, leaving the door open. Kārlis heard him say, "Oy-yoy-yoy. Kārlis ever been in a fight before?"

"I've hardly ever seen him without pen and paper in his hands," came the reply, sounding like Vilz.

"Me either," said someone else, probably Hugo.

Hmph. As if Hugo was such a bruiser, Kārlis fumed from his heap of mangled limbs. He could just picture Hugo and all the others standing around the kitchen, sharing knowing looks over cups of hot coffee about how they might have predicted Kārlis would be skunked.

"He'll be okay," Mr. Leopolds said. "But in the future, when I say don't do anything rash, this is exactly what I mean not to do. Need I be more specific? Don't pick fights with Russians. Don't go to secret meetings. Don't set off fireworks or otherwise attract attention to yourselves." He was speaking slowly, as if to idiots. "I thought these things were obvious."

"This would not have happened if it hadn't been for that spy the Pērkons have to quarter," Eriks said.

"We coulda handled him if Mr. Pērkons hadn't come in and stopped us," said a fast, high-pitched voice, Sniedze. "Mr. Pērkons wouldn't let us do nothing while that devil whipped the snot out of Kārlis. I mean he flogged Kārlis to a bloody pulp."

Kārlis moaned into his salt pillow.

"Thank God somebody with a brain came along," Mr. Leopolds said.

"But you shoulda heard Eriks stand up to the creep," Sniedze said. "Eriks said he better keep his mitts off his coat. That it was made of camel and herring and lots of other animals and he better keep his mitts off it."

"By the way, Sniedze," Eriks said, "in case I forget to mention it later, Shut Up. Why'd you tell that jerk my name?"

"What? I would never," Sniedze said. "On account of the Nonchalant code and all."

"The what?" Mr. Leopolds said. "What code?"

"You told him my family had the finest department store in Riga," Eriks interrupted. "That's the same as giving him my name."

"I doubt he could afford to shop there," Sniedze said, sounding bewildered.

"Something else, Mr. Leopolds," Eriks said. "This so-called apprentice, this Igor Volkov, he bragged about being at Kalnins Bridge & Iron before he came to Pērkons Leather. You think he had any connection to what happened to Peters?"

It was so quiet Kārlis thought he heard water dripping in the sink.

"I don't know," Mr. Leopolds said. "The forge was nationalized months ago. That didn't happen because of some punk spy. You're saying you think the NKVD was sent to pick up Peters? It wasn't just bad luck you ran into them sledding?"

"Yah. What if?" Eriks said. "What is it, Mr. Leopolds? What's that look mean?"

"Well, I went over to the Kalnins place this morning," Mr. Leopolds said, "I thought I ought to talk to Peters's parents on account of what happened yesterday. But the whole family is gone. According to a neighbor they were all taken somewhere."

"What? Yesterday?"

"Yah. And, well ... "

"What?"

"Apparently the NKVD gave Mrs. Kalnins quite a hard time."

Kārlis rolled up on an elbow, cocking his ear toward the kitchen. The gang was silent at this appalling news.

"Makes sense in a way," he heard Mr. Leopolds say. "They'd have to make it rough for a lady like that, to force her to say where her sons were."

Kārlis was chilled to the center of his soul.

"If that's what happened, maybe it wasn't a coincidence that Peters was picked up," Mr. Leopolds said. "Seems farfetched though. I don't think the NKVD is that organized. It's safe to say, though, that they have it in for all of us eventually."

"You think this Volkov turd informed on Peters's family," Eriks said, like he couldn't shake loose that idea.

"Maybe. We might never know what happened to the Kalninses. Personally, I didn't appreciate their politics, but God help them if the Cheka got a hold of them. A miserable year," Mr. Leopolds said. "Well, I'll be back shortly."

The back door to the alley shut and Kārlis heard the snap of locks.

The kitchen was silent. Kārlis sagged back, assuming everyone there, like him, was horrified by the image of mother-torture. Finally, it sounded like someone threw a log in the oven. A couple of dishes rattled.

"Kārlis is in no condition to do this." It was Hugo speaking. Kārlis recognized his debate-team-captain voice. "We should wait."

"Kārlis has already done his part," Vilz said. "We'll finish it without him."

"When?" Hugo said.

"Today," Vilz said.

"I don't think we're ready," Hugo said. "I mean, you did an ace job on the bottles, but we should practice with them. Let's go out to the summerhouse and light some in the woods. Besides, Kārlis's mother always has something to eat. We should take him there."

The thought of his mother's cooking made Kārlis's eyes moist.

"We only have four cocktails," Vilz said, walking into the pantry and flipping on the light again. Wearing her black bomber jacket and Greek sea captain's hat indoors made her look like she was ready to sabotage something that very moment. "If we light some in the woods then we won't have enough for the Corner House."

Hugo followed Vilz, saying, "If these things aren't handled with respect they'll blow your face off."

"Exactly. I say we blow off some Russian faces first," Vilz said. "Then we go out to Kārlis's and lay low."

Eriks filed in, followed by Jekabs. Kārlis felt oddly comforted to be surrounded by the gang, included in the conversation. His injuries couldn't be as minor as Mr. Leopolds suggested. He was due some honor.

Jekabs reached to the back of an upper shelf and lifted a small, wire-handled metal crate, positioning it gingerly on the center of the floor. "Ta da! They're bang-up professional, if I say so myself," he said flinging off a dishtowel covering.

Kārlis sensed a pressure change in the room. Rolling on his side, he put on his glasses and raised his head to see what everyone was looking at: four ominous milk bottles, the mouths stoppered tight with black electrical tape and wax, tidy fuses of ripped gold-fringed blanket hanging over their sides. The guys must've made and stashed them while he'd slept.

"Mixed in kerosene for added sticking power," Vilz explained, which explained the oily stink.

Kārlis drew away from the bottles, scrunching up on the shelf. These were lethal, the real deal.

"I think the Finns would approve," Vilz said. She closed the pantry door and took a deep breath. "Me and Eriks will take the upstairs windows. Jekabs and Hugo, chuck these in the ground floor or basement. Whatever seems most vulnerable. Then run like hell."

"Where to?"

"Not here," Jekabs said. "We can't lead the Cheka straight to Uncle Eli's door."

"Hugo, remember those elaborate escape routes you devised the time Eriks hoisted Ludvigs Circenis's bicycle up the flag pole?" Vilz said.

"You want to base our egress on that?" Hugo said.

"If egress means getaway, then, yah," Vilz said. "You studied traffic patterns and train schedules and you came up with those routes and alternates."

"Yah. Nothing's really changed," Hugo admitted. "Those would work."

"Well, we can't plan everything exactly," Vilz said. "But that gets us to the train station. Try to catch the last ride out to the Pērkons place. We'll call the mission a success when all of us have made it to Kārlis's."

Kārlis looked around the circle. They all seemed to be memorizing the looks of one another. Vilz's gaze rested on Sniedze. "Except for Sniedze," Vilz said. "His job will be to help Kārlis home right away."

"I don't need any help," Kārlis said.

"Yah, you do," Vilz said. "We all have a job, and that's Sniedze's."

Oh-ho! So that's your angle, Kārlis saw. Vilz was giving *him* a job, the crumby task of babysitting Sniedze during all the Corner House excitement. He tried to protest, but jolting rib pain shut his mouth. What the heck? If he went along with it, at least he would be lying on his mother's featherbeds instead of this hard shelf.

"That all right with you, Eriks?" Vilz said. "You still mad or something?"

"No. But I'm not going to meet you at Kārlis's," Eriks said. "If I'm going to lay low I want girls and a piano to be involved. Other than that, it's a good plan."

Vilz shrugged. "Suit yourself," she said.

Eriks reached down and lifted a Molotov cocktail from the crate, slipping it into his coat pocket like he handled them every day.

"You're taking that now?" said Hugo.

"Yah. But I can't firebomb anything on an empty stomach," Eriks said. "I'm going home to grab a bite. We have to wait 'til dark anyway. I'll see you in the park in an hour."

"Bring your lighter," Vilz said. "I only have matches."

"We're really going to do this," Hugo muttered.

"Bring me something to eat?" Sniedze said to Ers.

"Sorry," Eriks said, raising the wide lapels cʜɪs overcoat and turning to go. "I'm not adding ,ʰɪc-smuggling to the list of tonight's felonies."

"Be careful," Vilz said. "You really stand oɪ that light color, and as tall as you are. The NKʜ grab you, you know, just for looking spiffy."

Eriks put on his gloves, saying, "If being tall and debonair brings down the Cheka then let's face it, fellas, I'm a goner." He turned at the doorway, saying, "Next time I see you citizens, better have your shoes laced tight, because we'll be moving fast.

- 7 -

ERIKS STRODE DOWN THE MIDDLE of the alley, kicking a hunk of ice, worries itching like scratchy wool underwear. The worst was the fear that he'd endangered his family, Sniedze's blunder that divulged Eriks's family's business. *Dammit.* Now the name Gailis dangled like a fat mouse before a sadistic Igor Volkov cat.

Something else was becoming clear. Volkov was the common factor to a string of stinking events smashing up his world. The *kāpost galva* had practically bragged about destroying the Kalnins family. Then he'd gotten away with beating up Kārlis. Something had to be done about that sick weasel before he turned his deadly stone eyes toward Eriks's family. Eriks wanted to warn his parents right away.

He quickened his step.

After burning down the Corner House, he'd finish business with Igor Volkov. He couldn't do anything about this goliath Soviet occupation screwing with every aspect of his life, but he could do something about one Russian punk. And there would be nothing *nonchalant* about the way he planned to step on Volkov's neck, so he wouldn't tell the others. This time no one would be around to make him compromise or play it safe.

He'd do it for Peters, he thought, eyes welling up. And for Kārlis.

Eriks gauged the heft of the Molotov cocktail in his pocket. Then, looking around, he picked up a hunk of ice and heaved it at the blasphemous new street sign. Bullseye. That felt good. That's how he'd nail the Corner House window.

Brushing snow from his gloves, he turned out of the alley and strode down what used to be his favorite district of the city. Until a few months ago, a parade of swanky stores and restaurants had lined the boulevard here. Now most were dark inside or boarded up. It was depressing. The sidewalks were crowded with people in dark clothes, hunched over and hurrying, as if they wanted to be invisible.

Looming ahead on the next block was his father's department store, seven stories of elegant, mid-century art nouveau architecture dominating every corner of the block. When the light changed, Eriks crossed to it, saddened by the shabby presentation of a window full of empty cartons, its backdrop curtain bunched up and flipped over the rod. Window after dark window stared at him like empty eye sockets. Everything was dead. What the hell did the Communists do with all the Christmas decorations? They meant to destroy him, body and spirit. He saw that.

Crossing the street again, he put the store behind him.

Ahead on the sidewalk, a couple of NKVD agents stumbled out of a pub noisy with Russians. One looked smashed and Eriks reckoned he could snatch the guy's hat and disappear into the crowd before the brute felt his ears get cold. But he let the agent stagger away with his hat, saving his energies for the Corner House.

He crossed the esplanade, passed the Freedom Monument—keeping his distance as it was strictly off limits these days—and skirted Bastion Hill Park where Peters liked to sled. Was Peters really dead?

By the time Eriks reached the townhouse tears were dripping off his chin. The top floor windows were lit and he could hardly wait to be up there, telling his parents about everything. Dinner would be ready and his father and mother would be finishing the ritual cocktail at the window, admiring the onset of city lights.

Eriks ran up stone steps flanked by two giant, marble lions dusted with snow. He pushed open the glass door himself, hoping the doorman wouldn't see his red eyes.

"I've got the elevator, old man," Eriks said, unnecessarily. Old Topper seemed to be avoiding him anyway, probably still sore about Eriks's latest booby-trap heaping snow on his head. No one had a sense of humor anymore. Eriks closed himself in the elevator with a tug of the accordion-style iron gate and pushed the brass lever. The motor churned, rising floor by floor to the fifth, where it clanked to a stop at a deserted, oak-paneled vestibule.

The door to his home was open. Eriks went in, locking it behind him.

"Mama, I'm home."

Not stopping to remove his coat, he flung his fedora like a discus and proceeded directly to the sitting room. The view through the picture window always grabbed him. Lights from the Opera House, the Hotel Riga and the Art Academy glistened over the snow, with spires of the city skyline and the harbor cranes silhouetted faintly behind. But his parents were not there admiring it. The fire had been left to burn itself out. Father's whiskey poured, but not drank. Eriks downed a swig, glad his parents weren't there to see he'd been crying.

Going to the washroom, he extracted the Molotov cocktail from his pocket and set it on the counter, splashed water on his face and tried taming his hair. Then he plucked a sprig of holly from the flower arrangement, replacing the stale boutonniere in his lapel. When tears inexplicably came again he slumped against the wall, holding a towel over his face. After a couple of breaths, he wiped his eyes and nose and tossed the towel on the counter. Then he saw it.

In the corner of the mirror, written in red lipstick were the words, *Run Er—*.

The lipstick was broken off, the gold tube lying on the counter. It was his mother's. Barely breathing, he stretched his hand to the mirror and carefully rubbed the writing with a finger. The letters smeared creamy and red under his touch. Still staring dumbly, he heard pounding on the front door.

He stood motionless, as if unable to comprehend the meaning of the word before him. *Run*. Did it mean…? He locked the bathroom door, flew to the window and threw up the sash. Freezing air hit him as he sat on the sill and swung his legs through the window. Looking down at the inner courtyard central to the building, he paused thinking, *This is insane.*

When the front door crashed open, slamming into the wall, Eriks took his mother's advice.

He ran.

With one arm hanging onto the window frame, he swung as far as he could to the side, grabbing the drainpipes. His feet scrambled against the bricks as Eriks let go of the safety of the sill and clung to the vertical pipes with both hands. Fingers burned against the freezing pipes, but he held tight and began his descent.

He didn't look down. Already passing the windows of the downstairs neighbors, he didn't consider whether he could scale a five-story building. A gunshot thundered from his house and his drop became unthinking, a loosely tethered fall, skin scraping, stinging, skidding between the pipes and the wall.

A hard whizzing flick nicked his wool coat, echoing in a metallic ricochet around the courtyard. Eriks let go, plunging past the first-story into a pile of snow. He rolled off, sprang up and ran. In seconds he was out of the courtyard and running down the sidewalk. He pushed between an older couple in his path, darted around a cluster of impossibly slow figures, and sharply turned a corner before slowing to a stride, panting.

Was everyone looking at him? He didn't want to stand out, wanted to blend in with everyone. He tried to look like every other citizen rushing to be home by curfew, but his lungs screamed with every breath, hammers banging in his head. He needed to hide.

A streetcar was passing. Eriks loped into the street and sprang onto the back platform. He met the driver's eyes in a mirror, but the fellow didn't say anything. Seats were full so he clung to a pole until he noticed he was smearing blood all over it and hid his hands in his pockets.

People got off at a stop and Eriks took a seat, mind racing. What was happening? Where were his parents? What had he done? Resisted the NKVD? They killed people for that, for much less than that. They'd kill him. They'd already tried to kill him. He'd crossed a line. He couldn't go home. He'd be in danger there. He'd be a danger to anyone who helped him.

The trolley was emptying its passengers at each stop, making Eriks more and more conspicuous. *Blend in,* he thought, wishing he were invisible among those hunched in their dark coats, but with his mammoth frame, wild hair and bloody hands he stood out like the Yeti among villagers. His mind went numb as he frantically figured what to do.

He was headed in the exact opposite direction as Vilz and the others who waited for him at the Corner House. The Molotov cocktail! He'd left it on the bathroom counter! What an idiot he was! Now, if his friends did succeed in executing *his* stupidly, brazen plan, he'd just provided a tidy link between his family and the bombing of NKVD headquarters. His stomach cramped. He'd worry about that later. Right now, the streets were clearing. If he didn't get inside soon, he would be noticed and arrested for curfew violation.

A building at the end of the block looked familiar. He had once walked home a girl who lived there. Mentally ravaging the pages of his little black book, Eriks came up with the name Zelma. Zelma Barons. She'd been easy to talk to and before he'd known it he'd walked her all the way home one day after school. Zelma hadn't been very adventurous though when he'd returned that night and tossed pebbles at her third story townhouse window. He'd eventually abandoned hope of shenanigans with Zelma for the company of a game folk dancer. But the doorman might recognize Eriks and let him in the building. He just needed to get inside.

It was a shaky plan, Eriks admitted trying to tame his hair with his fingers. But in its favor was the fact that his family and friends didn't know Zelma. No one would be able to provide her name,

even under torture.

Where did *that* horrid thought come from? He shook it off and entered the townhouse foyer, scouting for the doorman.

Instead, Eriks met the last people he wanted to see.

The lobby was filled with the NKVD, identical in their long, green woolen coats, knee-high black boots, and caps bearing the shiny, red hammer-and-sickle badges. In every chair sat an agent. They stood in groups of three or four, chatting it up, drinking coffee and eating sandwiches. Some had sub-machine guns dangling at their sides. Eriks walked unwittingly into their midst, seen by them all.

"It's past curfew, punk," said a Chekist near the door. "Who are you?"

Eriks tried to appear calm.

The Chekist pushed him, knocking Eriks into the back of another agent who turned, acting highly insulted. "We don't want *that* walking around," the Chekist said, looking Eriks up and down. "Look at the size of its feet."

More Russians circled Eriks, looking eager for some entertainment.

A gloved hand slapped Eriks's face. "I said what's your name?"

His lips trembled. Is this how it had started for Peters? Eriks thought of the girl from school who lived in the building. "Barons," he said, using her name. "Eriks Barons."

"I can't think of one reason why I shouldn't arrest you right now, Eriks Barons. Let's see some identification."

He couldn't reveal his name, couldn't take his bloody hands from his pockets to feign reaching for a wallet. It's over already, Eriks thought, out of moves, caught in the closing circle of agents, suffocating.

"Eriks!"

Eriks jerked his head toward a huge, fair man in civilian clothes who pushed forward, barking at him.

Eriks had never before seen the giant Latvian, who squeezed between the NKVD and, to Eriks's shock, slapped him on both sides of the face, hard.

"You know not to miss curfew!" the man said, grabbing Eriks by his coat. "I've been looking all over for you. Your mother is hysterical." He shoved Eriks toward the stairway. "Get up there, boy, and get my belt."

Eriks stumbled away, hands in pockets, jaw jarred by the heavy-handed slaps. Aware that the man had pulled out papers, identifying himself to the NKVD, Eriks kept climbing and didn't look back.

"Augusts Barons, Comrade Officer. Worker at the People's Mill. You have my word the boy will never again be seen after curfew."

When Eriks reached the third-floor landing, a crack of light widened to reveal a lady on the other side. She had grayish-brown hair and the same slender build as his school-mate, Zelma. Probably waiting for her husband, surprise and suspicion crossed her face when she saw Eriks. Her eyes went wide when he stumbled over the threshold, Mr. Barons right behind him, but she closed the door swiftly, without a word.

Once inside, Eriks breathed. It felt like the first breath in an hour.

Mr. Barons leaned against the door, looking drained, pushing his hand against his forehead.

"Augusts, what's going on?" the lady said with a turn of shoulder meant to exclude Eriks. "Please don't tell me you stuck your neck out. They're watching us."

Mr. Barons's eyes were closed. He shook his head, still leaning against the door as if he was melting into the wood.

Eriks wiped his boots on the doormat, guiltily realizing the risk Mr. Barons had taken for him. "*Paldies.* Mr. Barons, I—"

"Forget it, son," Barons said quietly. "Got a nephew your age." The corners of his mouth turned down. "Been missing for two weeks. But we'll talk later. Right now, the Cheka."

Eriks watched curiously as Mr. Barons proceeded to remove his belt and wrap it around his hand. "They love violence," Barons said, "so let's give them plenty of pain."

Eriks nodded vaguely, without grasping Mr. Barons's meaning.

Suddenly Barons faced the door and shouted, "You're going to learn the importance of curfew tonight, boy. I'm going to beat the hell out of you."

Then Eriks realized it was for the benefit of any listening NKVD.

Drawing back his arm, Barons whipped the armchair with his belt.

It took Eriks a moment to realize he had a role to play in the charade.

He cried out as if he'd been lashed.

Again, Barons whipped the armchair.

"Aghh," Eriks cried, shook by the anger he saw in Mr. Barons's blows.

"That was nothing!" Barons bellowed toward the door. Then he said quietly to Eriks, "Who the hell are you?"

Whap!

Eriks screamed. Then he whispered, "Eriks Gailis. I go to school with your daughter. The Cheka came to my house tonight but I escaped out the window. It happened so fast. I don't know where to—"

Whap!

"Please, sir, that's enough," Eriks pleaded loudly, "I'll improve, I promise."

Mrs. Barons pressed her ear against the door. A moment later she turned to Mr. Barons, shaking her head.

"No, I don't think you've grasped the lesson yet," Barons called.

Whap!

The belt lashed the chair with a hide-splitting *smack*. A button popped off the upholstery.

"Please, sir, no more!"

Barons looked to his wife.

Holding up a finger to signal she was trying to listen, she whispered, "I think they went back downstairs."

Barons gestured for Eriks to have a seat. Mrs. Barons removed a stack of books from a doily-covered armchair.

Eriks sat down shakily, trying to calm his heartbeat while Barons uttered fatherly threats and threaded his belt through the loops around his waist. He looked around the small, simply furnished haven, remembering the night he'd tossed pebbles at Zelma's window. If he'd known then how Zelma's father handled a belt, he would never have risked it.

Mr. Barons peered down at Eriks, which knocked Eriks off balance as he was used to being the tallest person in a room. The man looked friendly, but insistent, like he expected an explanation. He was blue-eyed and, oddly for someone of his age, freckled.

Eriks squirmed, clutching his hair, which no doubt looked as out of control as he felt. Suddenly he panicked at what he'd done and didn't want to admit to Zelma's parents that he'd defied the NKVD. He didn't want to tell Zelma's parents someone had shot at him for fear they'd think him a criminal. Zelma's mother was looking at his hands, bloody from his escape. He stuffed them into his pockets.

"Our family store is Gailis & Sons," Eriks said. "You know it? The swanky department store?"

"I know it," Mrs. Barons said.

"That's our store. It was nationalized a while ago," Eriks said, suddenly confused. "My parents cooperated. I don't see why they came for us now."

As he spoke, Eriks's mind wandered, circling suspiciously around the ratfink, Igor Volkov. He hadn't snuffed the cancerous parasite, and see what happened. He'd nearly been treated to a first-hand tour of the Corner House. He reined his thoughts back to Zelma's parents who were looking dubiously at him, the liability they'd let in the door.

"You took a huge risk pretending to be my father, Mr. Barons," Eriks said, grateful.

Mrs. Barons turned sharply toward her husband. She wouldn't have endangered her family for a stranger, Eriks guessed.

"How will I be able to repay you?" Eriks said.

Mr. Barons walked to the window where he stood as if pondering the view, though the blinds were tightly shut. Finally, he turned back, telling Eriks, "You can't stay here."

Eriks was hugely disappointed to hear that. He couldn't even imagine where else he might go. And what about that lobby full of NKVD agents? Must he pass through that again?

"The building is crawling with informants," Barons said. "It's a favorite meeting place of the NKVD as you've discovered. So you can't stay here. You can't return home either. I do know of a place, however. Safest place I know, as a matter of fact. My own daughter is there. You'll have to come with me to the mill. I'm considered an *unreliable*, but I'm still the foreman. A train loaded with lumber will be leaving before dawn.

You should be on it."

"What about my parents?" Eriks said.

"They've probably been picked up," Barons said gently.

"Picked up?"

"Taken to the Corner House or the Central Jail," Barons said.

Aghast, Eriks fell into the armchair feeling faint.

"Some are loaded on trains to Moscow or points beyond," Barons said, in consolation.

Eriks felt like a storm-battered bird, blown off course, flying over the wreckage of what had been his life, seeking the remains of anything familiar, any landmark, somewhere he might alight for a moment's rest. All was gone.

"Believe me when I say your father wants you to run to safety, Eriks, not to go looking for them," Barons said. "If you want to repay me for helping you, then leave the city. Thank me by getting out of here alive."

- 8 -

THE TRAIN FROM RIGA WAS like riding thirty minutes in an icebox. Kārlis slouched on a seat in the back, disgruntled to be stuck with Sniedze while the other boys executed the glorious and defiant strike against the Corner House. Taking a folded paper from his pocket, Kārlis smoothed it out to examine a recent drawing: a caricature of Stalin, moustaches bigger than his arms, brandishing a trident and skewering skulls. He was pleased with the sketch, imagining an art critic reviewing his work with words like *Chilling* and *Evocative*. Inspired by the spires and castle walls growing smaller outside his window, he quickly drew in the iconic Riga skyline.

"Sheesh. I'd love a signed copy of that," Sniedze said, looking over Kārlis's shoulder. "One day when you're a famous artist—"

"Sniedze, I will throttle you if you ever mention my name in connection with a drawing," Kārlis said. "In fact, never mention my name, period. For any reason. *Ak tu kungs.* Sometimes I wish I didn't even know you." Kārlis wished he hadn't said that last part out loud. It wasn't true. It was just that he felt so crumby, being beat up and sent home to Mother.

They spoke little for the remainder of the trip.

Medieval architecture gave way to warehouses, then to silos and farms and finally, to forests. Kārlis hid his injuries by wearing his fedora low and his muffler high, like the Invisible Man in the movie poster. But he was still scared when he got off at the village and had to walk right by an armed NKVD guard, whose raised rifle barrel dominated the platform.

He can't read my mind, Kārlis assured himself. He doesn't know I've collaborated to firebomb his headquarters, or that his supreme commander is the butt of my drawing. Intimidated, Kārlis abandoned a notion he'd entertained all day of poking his head in the Bier Schtube to say *sveiks* to Lileja Lipkis. *Ak tu kungs*, it had been awkward enough during peacetime to come up with some plausible excuse to visit her. But now with that NKVD agent lurking about no one in his right mind would go to a pub, much less drink beer with neighbors.

Kārlis looked at the tavern's curtained windows, imagining what Lileja was doing behind them. Maybe she was peeking out in hopes Kārlis walked by. Maybe Mr. Leopolds was right about girls finding his injuries really attractive. Kārlis raised a bandaged hand to his fat lip. Ow.

"Hey, I just thought of something," Sniedze said. "We could go by the Bier Schtube and say *sveiks* to Lileja."

Kārlis stumbled midstep, taken aback, dismayed that Sniedze's mind ran parallel to his, especially where Lileja was concerned. "That's an exceedingly stupid idea, Sniedze."

"Why? She might give us some more cake," Sniedze said.

"What do you mean?"

"Last time I went there with Hugo she gave us some cake. Want to go?"

Suddenly hot and prickly, Kārlis tore the muffler away from his neck. "*Hugo* has been calling on Lileja? That white-faced traitor! He might have had the guts to mention it."

Sniedze looked at him expectantly. Kārlis could practically see the slices of cake in his shining eyes.

"I'm going to visit Lileja later," Kārlis said. "But I don't think you should be with me, no offense."

There was a proper way to court a lady. It was not with Sniedze in tow. And it wasn't with bloodshot eyes swollen shut. He would wait until the bruises and swelling had gone down. Do things in the proper order. That was Kārlis's motto. There was no rush. He said, "I haven't even told her yet that I've been accepted to the Art Academy."

Sniedze shrugged. "I'm pretty sure Hugo told her about that."

Kārlis stopped walking, appalled. Hugo had stolen a moment from him.

"Hugo doesn't know the first thing about the Art Academy," Kārlis snapped, feeling hollow. His hand went to his wallet, the matriculation card. He could still wow Lileja with that.

Fifteen minutes of walking warmed Kārlis's limbs and brought him to the turn where a long driveway led to the Pērkons's summerhouse and the river beyond. Kārlis had expected to see the place lit up and Christmas cheery, to see the colored glass around the front door glowing like jewels. Instead, the big-stoned building receded into the twilight, windows dark, as if it were hiding behind its flanking linden trees. The driveway hadn't been shoveled and it occurred to Kārlis that might be deliberate.

"Hold it. Let's go around the back," Kārlis said. "No sense making a trail of footprints leading to the front door."

Sniedze followed him on a circuitous route through trees. Then they skirted the stone walls to reach the front door, which was locked.

Kārlis knocked while they banged snow off their boots.

The curtain parted, framing the round eyes, round face and straight braids of his little sister. "You look like ground beef," Biruta said, opening the door. "What does *compulsory service* mean?"

"Hello to you, too. Where's Mother?" Kārlis said, shedding his coat and detecting a tantalizing aroma.

From the other side of the dining room, Kārlis saw Tante Agata's gray head emerge from the kitchen, her hand at her throat. His banging at the door must have frightened the old bird. Seeing it was Kārlis she turned back to whatever she was doing that filled the house with such savory warmth.

"Wanna light matches?" Biruta asked Sniedze.

"Okay," he said, following her to the fireplace.

Kārlis went to the kitchen where his elderly aunt stood at the sink skinning potatoes. Zeita, the house cow, was nearby, her gentle brown head lowered in a bucket of grain.

"Something smells good," Kārlis said, groaning with relief at the warmth and promise of dinner. "I'm starving."

Tante Agata scanned Kārlis from head to toe with pursed lips as if she'd seen plenty of bloodied up boys before and he was nothing special. "I'm going to put some meat on your bones if it's the last thing I do," she said.

The trap door to the root cellar was open and Kārlis could hear someone rummaging around down there. "*Sveiks*, Mama," Kārlis said, bending over the opening.

"Kārlis! Oh, Karli, we just heard," came his mother's voice. "I'm so glad you've come. Are you okay?"

"Not bad, Mama. Bastard caught me off guard that's what happened." He answered Tante Agata's dubious gaze saying, "It was not a fair fight at all." The old lady seemed to be comparing his wounds to her pharmacy of dried herbs hanging from the rafter.

"I was caught off guard as well," called his mother amid the clanking of jars. "Frankly, I'm in shock."

"News travels fast," Kārlis said. Wait. How was it even possible? The fight, if he could call it that, just happened last night. There was no telephone here.

"We're cooking your favorite meal," she called up. "Roast pork and potatoes. Herring in cream."

"And black peas with pig snouts," said Tante Agata.

"Who told you about it?" Kārlis called down the cellar. He would've rather presented his own version of the confrontation with Volkov.

"Just—the telegram," his mother's voice grew louder as she trudged up the stairs. "Wasn't very informative though, was it?"

"What telegram?" Kārlis asked, thoughts jumping erratically to the Art Academy.

"It said you had to report right away for a medical exam," she said. "I'm so glad you came home first."

His mother's head and shoulders rose into the kitchen, the light brown hair, swirled and mounded on top of her head, the puffy, starched sleeves of her blouse. When she turned to face him, he saw she'd been crying, gray eyes ringed in pink. Not only that, she was clearly stunned by his battered condition. Eyebrows frozen in arches, she stared at his face aghast. "What happened to you?"

Kārlis leaned down to take the basket of potatoes from her hands.

"What telegram, Mama?"

She pointed at the table where a formal-looking missive leaned against the salt grinder. Kārlis took the notice, reading it quickly.

"You've been called up," his mother said, dabbing her nose with her handkerchief, "by the Red Army."

He read it again.

Then a wrecking ball let loose, demolishing his inner edifice. Closing his eyes, Kārlis saw the carefully planned future crash, the dust of confusion billowing thick.

A call-up notice. He couldn't breathe. They'd make him be a soldier in his enemy's army. His future lay in the hands of some old man with rows of medals who wanted to impress Stalin. He gasped. So many things he'd been worrying about didn't matter anymore.

When Kārlis opened his eyes, Zeita's big head was looming over him, her huge brown eyes suggesting she might treat him to a tongue-grooming.

"Raspberry leaves and Lady's Mantle," Tante Agata said, a bony finger in the air. "I'll make an infusion." Eyeing his stripes, she added, "and a tincture."

"Good idea," his mother said. "Kārlis, do you want to lie down?"

"No. Not really," Kārlis said, scratching Zeita behind the ears and settling into a kitchen chair. He felt weirdly energized and calm after reading the telegram. He just wanted to sit here. He wanted to watch his mother cook dinner. He wanted to notice every detail, because one thing was for sure. He'd be leaving here. He rested the side of his head on an outstretched arm, absently smoothing the red woven tablecloth to its edges.

His mother went to the window, pulled up a corner of the curtain and looked out. Snow was piled all the way up to the windowsill. Putting her face near the glass, she craned her neck looking in all directions. Daylight was fading fast. The glass was steamy and beaded with moisture from the cast iron teapot bubbling on the woodstove and the pork roasting in the coal-fed oven.

"Darkest day of the year," his mother murmured, tucking the thick curtain back around the glass.

"Solstice," said Tante Agata. She reached a bony old arm above her head, toward bundles of herbs she'd wildcrafted on Midsummer Day and procured in obscure stalls of the Central Market. "The dark triumphs, but only briefly," she said, snapping off a sprig.

Kārlis felt mesmerized and restful watching her rub the herb between her fingers, green flakes falling in a square of cheesecloth.

"The coming days gradually get brighter," Tante Agata said, shrewd blue eyes looking over a sparrow nose at Kārlis. "How many are we for dinner, Anna?"

"Sniedze's here," Kārlis said, suddenly remembering. "And the boys might come by." The Nonchalants's urgent scheme of one hour ago was now remote and irrelevant. How long did he have left before he was shipped somewhere, and approved by the medical examiner to be healthy Latvian cannon fodder?

"How nice," his mother said. "Good for you to be with your friends— Oh! I forgot to mention ... " Her face sagged, revealing a weariness before she quickly disguised it with the flex of her smile, saying, "The Kruminses will be staying with us."

"Hugo's family?" Kārlis said.

"Yah. As is happening to everyone, they have been displaced. A Soviet officer moved into their apartment. So, until they get—well, for now, they are staying here."

"People must always welcome persons visiting their home on *Kekatas*," Tante Agata said, as if they were celebrating a solstice tradition, not struggling beneath a military occupation.

"So Hugo will be sharing your room," his mother said. "That's a spot of cheery news for you!"

"Oh joy," Kārlis said, dropping his forehead to the table. How convenient that would make it for Hugo to call on Kārlis's girl.

A hot cup of tea was set next to him. He drank it in gulps and more was poured. Dreams and nightmares swirled together and vanished with its vapors. The women's voices droned indistinctly. Elza will sleep on a cot ... guest bedroom for Hugo's parents. It will be a squeeze. Will you spoon the cream over the filets? Janis won't be home in time for dinner, but that still makes ten.

Everything was blown out of order. And Kārlis was out of time. He'd better go see Lileja.

"I'll peel more potatoes," said Tante Agata.

- 9 -

THE INDOMITABLE SIX-STORY HOUSE ON the corner had been a lavish apartment building prior to housing NKVD headquarters. Its ornate facade presented rows of iron-edged balconies, jutting out under arched porticoes spiked with icicles and backlit by the yellow light of interior chambers. The balconies looked very much to Vilz like the centers of a target. A target she could hit, she decided, flexing her right arm and realizing she hadn't even played basketball since the occupation. Afraid of meeting the eye of a guard, Vilz returned her gaze to her feet traversing the sidewalk. The NKVD presence here was intense, a swarm of red hammer-and-sickle cap badges and tall black boots, gun barrels sticking out from the balconies at cockeyed angles, aiming at the moon or down at the scurrying citizens.

Jekabs leaned over, speaking out of the corner of his mouth. "Notice," he said, referring to someone ascending the steps to the Corner House. "All anyone has to do, if they don't like someone, is walk in that lobby and report them to *those who need to know.*"

"My mother says that's the tallest building in Riga," Hugo said, his voice stilted, laboring to talk over chattering teeth. "Because you can see Siberia from there." He'd hidden his white hair beneath a dark wool cap under his fedora, so he wouldn't be recognized as yesterday's fugitive.

"Very funny. But I'm not walking by that fortress of doom again," Jekabs said. They'd passed the Corner House twice in forty-five minutes looking for Eriks. "Gives me the heebie-jeebies."

"It has chinks," Vilz said. "Small weaknesses. We just have to find one."

"I swear that third floor guard is watching me," Jekabs said.

"They're changing all the time," Vilz said. "I think most of them are just out there to smoke."

"This is stupid," Jekabs said, as they crossed the street a block away and lingered with the commuters at a bus stop. "He's not coming."

Hugo said, "The longer we wait for Eriks, the emptier the street gets and the more we stand out."

The initial excitement that had surged as Vilz and the boys marched up Lenin Boulevard, each with a bottle-bomb hidden in a pocket, had peaked when the despised Corner House first loomed into view. But the optimism rapidly ebbed as they walked disorganized laps up and down the block looking, to no avail, for Eriks. Vilz was afraid that by now the verve needed to execute the ploy had leaked away entirely.

"Yah, but it's quickly getting darker, too," Vilz said, hoping to bolster their resolve, "which is in our favor."

"We're going to miss the last train before curfew if we don't get going," Hugo said.

"Face it, he's not coming," Jekabs said. "And if we

keep walking around looking for him one of those guards is going to notice us."

"Doesn't make sense," Vilz said. "This whole thing was his idea."

The three of them stood with their shoulders together, clustered within a larger crowd of folks waiting at the bus stop. Raising her head, Vilz looked around. Everyone seemed to be minding his own business.

"So, do it without Eriks?" Jekabs said, rubbing his hands together.

"Guess we'll have to," said Vilz, also stretching and flexing fingers, keeping her throwing hand warm.

"Nay," Hugo said. "This changes things. We ought to rethink it."

"Doesn't matter whether we fling three bottles or four," Vilz said. "But if we fling zero, then we've failed."

"Don't you think we ought to find out what happened to Eriks?" Hugo said.

"How we gonna do that? What if he decided to go dancing or—met a girl," Jekabs said. "I picture him somewhere—what was it he said? Laying low with girls and a piano, the bum."

"He wouldn't do that," Vilz said.

"If he did I'll pound the numbskull," Jekabs said. "Leaving us hanging like this."

"He wouldn't do that to us," Vilz said. "Maybe something made him late."

"What if it's something terrible?" Hugo said. "Shouldn't we see if he's at home? If he's all right?"

"Then we miss our chance here," Jekabs said. "We risked making these things and bringing them here for nothing."

"I agree," Vilz said. "Let's do what we came for. Then hunt Eriks down."

"But what if something did happen to him," said Hugo. "What if … what if he's in there?" Hugo nodded at the Corner House.

Vilz didn't want to hear that. "That's a stretch. That would be an unlikely coincidence."

"Yah, but it's possible," Hugo said. "In fact, I'm starting to think that's exactly what happened. You said yourself, it makes no sense he's not here. What if he got picked up?"

"Hugo, there could be a million other explanations why he's not here."

"Like what?"

They looked at each other.

Vilz sighed with exasperation.

"We should find out what happened to Eriks before we do anything," Hugo said. "That's the thing to do."

"But if he was arrested," Vilz said. "If he is in there. Isn't this what he would want? One of our cocktails to come sailing through a window so he could escape in the blazing chaos."

"I don't know," Hugo said, looking sober. "You could be right about that. I don't know what goes on in there. If people are locked up they might be trapped."

Vilz straightened and scanned the line of bus riders. No one appeared to be listening, but she leaned over so only Hugo and Jekabs could hear her. "The only thing Russians understand is violence. If we don't make it painful for them to occupy this place they'll never go away. We can't worry about hurting people."

"I worry about it if it's Eriks," Hugo said.

Vilz looked up and down the street, trying to remember how the fellow at the meeting worded it. A few blocks up, the bus was coming. She said, "This is the moment when we each have to decide: Are you okay living like this? Military occupation, curfew, not trusting anyone, every day until you die, while the world looks the other way, as if your death was nothing?"

"What is that, some kind of rhetorical question?" Jekabs asked, planting his feet. His folded, beefy arms looked tight under his coat.

"We didn't even practice with these things," Hugo said. His beanie dwarfed the refined features of his pale face. "Now that we see how it is, we should come back another time when we're organized."

Vilz mentally regrouped, imagining the fellow at the meeting. "So? Are we just going to get used to it?" she asked. "Until after a while, it's the normal state of things. Or is the way we used to live worth fighting for?"

Hugo pulled his collar up. He shoved his hands in his pockets with a shiver.

"Another thing," Jekabs said, looking annoyed. "Eriks was supposed to bring the lighter. Without that we only have matches. Takes two people to light one using matches."

"They've taken everything, but we still have the power to refuse to cooperate," Vilz persisted. "But it's vital that we act, and not rely on hope alone." The spiel sounded canned, even to Vilz. She couldn't summon the right words, the ones that tapped into the horrendous vein of rage flowing under her skin. Surely they knew the feeling, too. Crushing anger. Hatred that burned up everything you once liked about yourself. Fear you'd forget you ever knew the heights of life because you're always squirming under Russian boots. Hands always tied and never able to speak. Vilz clenched her fists, lips tight, unable to say what she meant.

The Corner House gloated at her from across the boulevard.

"Words and articles are great but—hell." Vilz looked around. She felt cloistered in the stream of head-down sidewalk-pounders. "Light me up, Jekabs."

Jekabs's head shot up, eyes darting around.

"If you don't want to do it, I understand," Vilz said. "Just give me a light."

Vilz's hand shook badly lifting the bottle bomb from her pocket. Holding it low before her, she feared the glass would slip from her sweaty palms and blow off all their heads.

Hugo fidgeted backward, probably thinking the same.

Jekabs stepped to face her. Bending slightly to shield the bottle with his squared shoulders, he struck the match.

Flame at the fuse, Vilz's right arm ejected the bottle immediately, arcing forcefully toward the second story portico. The Molotov cocktail flew off her fingers so fast, she was afraid the fabric wick had not caught fire. But before her hand was back in her pocket, glass crashed against the wall behind the balcony. An instantaneous *whoosh* of combustion drowned a man's scream.

Jekabs launched his bottle hard and true. And ran.

Hugo had long since vanished.

Jekabs's bomb punched with a blazing flashover. Twenty-foot flames and a spewing column of black smoke engulfed the portico. Vilz knew running would attract attention, but she could not control the voltage in her legs.

Distance from the Corner House was swiftly attained. Muscles fleet, senses charged, the corners and passages of her city opened before Vilz in gratitude. The bombs blasted with more power than she'd dreamed. The collective gasp of the bus crowd, the scream and shouts of confusion, all echoed in her head like harmonizing voices in a hymn of praise. Some lightness better than oxygen lifted from her lungs, perhaps hope or dignity. *Good God, what had she done?* She had to do this again.

K. Smiltens, 1946.

Epilogue

MEMORIES CHASED KARLIS PERKONS *down the forest path. Nike running shoes stepped quick, still pursued by Igor Volkov even though his nemesis lay in the root cellar, a shovel at his crushed skull.*

A lifelong wish for justice granted, the Russian colonist was dead. Kārlis wouldn't be the only one glad about that. After 1940, every Nonchalant hated the heart-shaped face that made the Russian occupation personal. Most every Latvian became a fervent enemy of the Soviet regime that year. But today the police would not dig any deeper than Kārlis to collar their culprit. He needed his lawyer. He readied his sixty-eight year old legs to race to the Bier Schtube telephone before the running footfalls from behind caught up.

A tug came from low, on his sports jacket hem. Chest thumping, Kārlis turned, seeing at first nothing but slashes of tree trunks against silver dusk. Then dropping his eyes to the blond head of his grandnephew, he was flooded with relief. It was just the boy, tugging at his coat and speaking in a rush.

He turned his good ear toward the round face.

"Uncle Kārlis, the police are looking for you," Johnny blurted. "About that body in the basement. I know I wasn't supposed to go down there. I'm sorry. I was digging for the treasure."

Kārlis nodded, again searching the woods before settling on Johnny's lively blue eyes. It was to be expected, he reckoned with a deep exhale. Bedtime tales of the family history had lodged in the boy's fertile imagination. Kārlis had planted them there himself. The boy had pestered him for a shovel ever since they'd arrived in Latvia, obsessed with plunder.

Bang! The sky cracked. Kārlis flinched. Just fireworks, Midsummer festivity, not bursting artillery like the last time he was in these woods. But it unnerved him.

"Johnny, let's not get hung up on the treasure."

"But the stories are true, you said so."

"Yah, of course. But it's also true that the Russians leave nothing, especially that one who is..." Kārlis raised an arm in the direction of the summerhouse, "...dead...in the cellar."

"Somebody killed that man." Johnny was spitting with excitement. "On purpose! Who would do it?"

Kārlis said nothing, imagining all who would line up behind him to dance on Volkov's grave. "Johnny you should go back—"

"No, I'm staying with you! There's a murderer on the loose," Johnny whispered fervently. The boy's imagination was kindled to a blaze, the widening blue eyes on a manhunt in the murky woods.

"There's no need to be afraid, muzais puisits," Kārlis said, though he also searched the trees for unwanted intruders, especially the police. "The world is safer with Volkov dead."

Kārlis felt at home in these woods, which Russians were reputedly afraid to enter. The boy would be in no danger if he stayed. "Come with me," Kārlis said, reaching out. Taking his grandnephew's smaller hand in his made a certain sense of the whole crazy imbroglio. And Johnny's presence inspired a side trip. "I want to show you something," Kārlis said. "It will only take a moment." Following his gut instinct felt as vital to Kārlis now as reaching his lawyer had been a moment before. "There's a giant oak over here, the granddaddy of the forest. You'll never see another one like it in your life."

Kārlis soon discovered that the path engraved on his memory no longer existed. He and Johnny were forced to tramp single file, unable to take even five steps in any direction without having to stop and swipe at an occupied spider web suspended at face level, or negotiate a fallen log, a knee-deep bog, and shoulder-high ferns. But the riverbank was right where he expected it to be, the high Midsummer sun glistening on its current.

"The tree should be up ahead. I remember we had a swing there in the spring."

"Uncle Kārlis?"

"Yah?" Kārlis turned his good ear toward the lad.

"Why bother to get the house back if the treasure's not even there?"

"For YOU, muzais puisits," Kārlis said, feeling indignant. "And for your grandchildren." He followed a deer trail that rose and dipped pleasantly through the rushes. "That's what my father intended."

"Maybe he hid it so good, the Russians didn't find the treasure."

Kārlis stopped. The boy's imagination was exceeded only by his optimism. "Johnny, if you could've seen this place when your great-grandfather owned it, you would know. All has been taken."

The slim shoulders fell under the little windbreaker.

Kārlis felt bad to dash the boy's hopes. "He was an optimist, too, my father," Kārlis said, in consolation. "You're his namesake, Johnny. And today is your Names Day. You and my father, your names come from Janus, the Roman god of the entrance and the exit, of looking ahead and looking behind. A very suitable name for my father. Everyone knew when Papu came into the room." Kārlis stumbled in time for a dizzying moment, picturing his towering father as a young man, much younger than Kārlis was now.

"Jānis Pērkons was a man of big ideas," Kārlis said, trying to stuff the past back in its grave and marshal his thoughts to the current problem of staying out of jail. "Everything in the proper order," he murmured, reassuring himself. But even his organizing mantra did not dispel the feeling that he was on the wrong track, missing something, the big picture.

"I'm sorry I went in the root cellar," Johnny said. "It's my fault the police are after you."

"Ak tu kungs, this is not your fault!" Kārlis said. He lowered himself to his haunches, to the level of the mushrooms on the boggy forest floor, to convince the child eye-to-eye of one sure truth. "These events were set in motion long ago, Johnny. I've waited a lifetime to set things right."

Notice

This story is inspired by the eyewitness accounts of
Kārlis Smiltens and Biruta Smiltens Mathur.

Georgia Saroj Mathur designed the book cover,
map, family tree and more.

Thank you Mathur Family, especially Kris, Anna, Georgia
and Walter--who insisted on digging for the treasure.

The help of Kārlis Smiltens, Barbara Peterson,
Al Martinez, Andrew Moore, Pauls Kesteris,
Lori Precious, Kathie Gibboney, Neal Mathur and
Gretchen Holzhauer-Irwin has been essential.

Shelly Youngren's critique group (Daniel Bradler,
Katherine Friedman, Sue Funkhouser, Barry Gilfry,
Marina Gutman, Don Pequinot, Cecelia Pitts, and
Alexander Rosenberg) made this readable.

The "Kansas Latvians" Arijs and the late Anta Krievins
contributed riveting recollections.

Paldies, James Mathers, Rodeo Grounds Poet Laureate.
Love to the irregulars at Café Mimosa.

K. Smiltens, 2000.

Diana Mathur, MBA cum homeschooling mother of three, has been privileged to travel to Latvia to research primary sources, collaborate closely with the de facto War Artist of the Latvian Legion, reclaim a summerhouse confiscated by Soviet-era communists, dig up treasure hidden in Latvian soil for fifty years, and travel the trans-Siberian railroad to what's left of the gulag archipelago on the trail of Stain-era deportees. The Mathurs live in California.

Bibliography

The following resources are acknowledged: *The Unknown War, The Latvian National Partisans Fight Against the Soviet Occupiers, 1944-1956* by Gunārs Blûzms et al, HPT Ltd., 2011, *Latvian Religion, An Outline*, Jānis Dārdedzis, Baltic Crossroads, Los Angeles, 1996, Museum of the Occupation of Latvia, *Latvia in World War II Catalogue-Guidebook of the Latvian Military Museum* by Valdis Kuzmins, *The Forgotten War, Latvian Resistance During the Russian and German Occupations* by Janis Straume, *Baltic Amber* by Inara Mantenieks, *Latvian Legion* by Arthur Silgailis, *Memoires of a Partisan* by Y. Sigaltchik, *In the Partisan Detachment* by Shmuel Margolin, *Laima Veckalne's Story: A Tale of Forgotten Soviet Crimes* by Edgar B. Anderson, *M16: Inside the Covert World of Her Majesty's Secret Intelligence Service* by Stephen Dorril, *Latvia: Year of Horror* by Baigais Gads, *Latvia in the Wars of the 20th Century* by Visvaldis Mangulis, *Hitler versus Stalin* by Professor John & Ljubica Erickson, *Landscape as an Indicator of Art Life in Latvia During the Period of Nazi Occupation* by Janis Kalnacs, www.cyberussr.com by Hugo S. Cunningham, *Occupation of Latvia by Nazi Germany, Forest Brothers* and *Baltic Way* by Wikipedia, *2X2 Divisions* by Frank Gordon from www.centropa.org, *Latvian Legion at Lake* ILMENA from www.lacplesis.com, Welcome to Latvia-Folk Songs from the Latvian Institute, www.li.lv, *These Names Accuse—Nominal List of Latvians Deported to Soviet Russia* by The Latvian Foundation, and *The Baltic Observer* since 1996 known as *The Baltic Times*.

Diligent effort has been made to acknowledge sources correctly. Any errors or unintentional omissions will be corrected in future editions of this book.

Glossary

Ak tu kungs! (AWK-te KOONKS) Oh my Lord! Give me patience!

Baltics Countries surrounding the Baltic Sea: Lithuania, Latvia, Estonia, and also Finland.

Bier Sctube A *bier stube* is a hall or pub that specializes in beer, German. In the story, Bier Schtube is a proper noun, and purposely misspelled to clue readers to its pronounciation.

Bolshevik Russian political party that embraced Lenin's Communist thesis

Cheka Another name for the NKVD

Corner House NKVD headquarters in Riga. In 1940, 700 "Undesirables" at a time were secretively incarcerated in the fashionable art nouveau building.

Проклятье Curse, an imprecation that great harm or evil may befall someone, *Proklyat'ye*, Russian

Daugava (DOW-guh-vuh) Latvia's longest river, running through Riga to the Baltic Sea

Я учусь на русском, товарищ I am/learning Russian, Comrade; *YA uchus' na russkom, tovarishch*, Russian

Kakis (KAT-kis), Latvian for cat and the name of Biruta's cat

Kāpost galva (KAP-ust GAUL-vuh) Stands for vulgar, teenaged slang. Use your imagination.

Kekatas Winter solstice mumming custom

Lats (LOTS) Latvian currency

Loudzu (LEWDZ-u) Please, and You're Welcome

Midsummer Summer solstice, revered and raucous Latvian holiday

Muzais puisits (MUZ-ice PWEE-seets) Little boy

NKVD Abbreviation for Narodnyi Komissariat Vnutrennikh Del, The People›s Commissariat for Internal Affairs, i.e. the Communist secret police, later known as the KGB

Name's Day The day of the year to celebrate a particular name and its bearers

Paldies (paul-DEE-es) Thank you

Pie joda (PEE-eh YO-duh) To the devil

Red Army Army of Russia, the Soviet Union

Riga (REE-guh) Capital of Latvia

Стой, или вы будете расстреляны! Stop, or you will be shot!, *Stoy, ili vy budete rasstrelyany*, Russian

Article 58

Sveiks (SVAYkes) Hello and See you later

The Pērkonses: It's only a matter of time, but being optimists, they always hope for one more day.

The Linden Tree & the Legionnaire

Witch Hammer

Diana Mathur

SMILTENS 1945

Book II: Witch Hammer
Available through Barnes & Noble.com, Amazon,
and wherever books are sold.

Book III: The Knock at Night

Available through Barnes & Noble.com, Amazon,
and wherever books are sold.

The Ghastly Year, Books I - III
Available through Barnes & Noble.com, Amazon,
and wherever books are sold.

Coming Soon!

Made in the USA
Las Vegas, NV
30 September 2023

78359482R00081